THE EDGE OF DOOM

The Edge of Doom

LEO BRADY

E. P. DUTTON & COMPANY, INC.
NEW YORK : 1949

AMERICAN BOOK–STRATFORD PRESS, INC., NEW YORK

FOR ELEANOR

Love alters not with his brief hours and weeks,
But bears it out even to the edge of doom.

—WILLIAM SHAKESPEARE, SONNET 116.

Contents

PART I   *THE DEED*   9

II   *THE THOUGHT*   59

III   *THE WORD*   203

I

The Deed

I

MARTIN watched the rain peck away at the window for
a long while without moving, almost without thinking;
watched the uneven lines of drops trace crooked paths down
the pane—like tears. When it stopped at last—when the beat
became inconstant and the globules looked white-bellied
and moved slowly and jerkily, he was aware that darkness was gradually smothering up against the glass from
both sides. It would be disrespectful, he felt, to turn on
the light. The body on the bed found hospitality in the
dark; death and darkness shared a community even before the tomb.

How long ago had his mother gurgled and sucked at
a stubborn word and relaxed completely? Two hours?
Three? Emptiness was impossible to measure. The echo
of her choke, her subsiding, weary groan had lingered
round the room for a long time: among the heavy drapes
that separated the two rooms, against the cracked ceiling,
along the splintered floor. Even it had died away finally,
leaving no record of her vain attempt to speak. She who
had been patient and seldom-spoken in life had sought to
exchange words with death and been denied. Was it, he
wondered, death's rattle? the straining word clicking

11

against the teeth and going guttural in the suddenly breathless throat?

He could barely see her now; it was memory and an indefinable sense that traced for him her outline on the old brass-headed bed. The stiff springs would creak no longer under the sparse weight; he recalled tenderly the warmth and friendliness of their squeak in the restless, haunted nights. She would toss no more now.

The rain ceased entirely now and the silence was complete, adding another dimension of emptiness to the room. He could suddenly not bear the hollowness. He rose in a lurch to discover that his legs were numb. Stiffly he moved into the next room and flicked on the light there, the stomp and rustle of his movements a balm to his muscles, a distraction to his grief. He came back and stood beneath the draperies to look at death in the faint spray of light that painted his shadow on the floor between himself and the bed.

Death had come to her after the steam of a two weeks' fever which hollowed her cheeks and labored her breathing. Yesterday the doctor—a spare, hopeless man more like a herald of death than a harbinger of life—had peered at the withered frame and shaken his head. His nervous hands seemed even then to perform ceremonial rites in preparation for the end. He had taken hope out the door with him when he left. Today when Martin offered a glass of water to the narrow lips, his mother had waved a hand feebly, choked and slobbered, essayed the word that never came, and died. No last words for her. No legendary wisdom to pass along to awed grandchildren. Not even a brave smile. She had gone out in pale, protesting incomprehension—as she had lived. Death had come in key, drab and colorless, with no spectacular chord to pomp its arrival. She was disappointed and helpless as in life—the blank monotony consistent to the end.

There were, he told himself, things to be done. Arrangements to be made, people to be informed—it was only then that he thought of the priest. Into his mind rocketed the realization that he had made no move toward summoning a minister of the Last Sacraments; it was a Presence in the room that would have provided some touch of pageantry. Her eyes might have thanked and colored, the word might have come clear; she might have gone in gallantry and gratitude. But he had trained himself not to think of the priests. And there had been no time anyway, he reassured himself, in the minutes between the warning and the event. And the priest wouldn't have come in a hurry—not to them; not when it meant tramping up the dingy three flights to the cave of their degradation. He knew them well enough for that. The Church's grand and precise rituals were designed to be acted out against more splendid backgrounds than his mother's gloomy brace of rooms. He remembered the grimness of Father Kirkman's face the other time—when he had gone to him to plead a favor—when he and his mother had gone together to the rectory and sat miserably in the parlor waiting for the refusal. If he had forgotten now, it was their fault, not his. He dismissed the guilt which presented itself inquiringly to his brain.

But he'd see to it that they gave her a good funeral. The shame and silence of her last moments could be repaid with some manner of splendor; she might have at least the grace of an expensive funeral. He'd make them give her that, he thought hotly, and imagined himself standing opposite a submissive priest, dictating his conditions. He had seen how the rich died: the parade of automobiles, the police escort, the solemnly-phrased eulogy, the expansive plot. If it was difficult for the rich man to enter in, it was the Church's habit to provide everything possible from this end—he curled his lip bitterly. He could ask that the same honors be paid his mother—she who had known poverty and despair in life was entitled at least to the irony of this attention in death. He had not the money, of course, to make even a pretense toward an expensive funeral; but the priest could provide it—if the will was there; he had been an altar boy: he had seen the elaborate vestments, the golden implements, the Monsignori in their long cars. He would ask for it at once; he would do his best, as some slight restitution for the deep lines which life had cut in the face and death accentuated, the strain which death had tightened.

He crossed the room hesitantly, as though he were in fear of waking the body, and patted his mother tenderly on the cheek. The chill of the skin shocked him and he drew back his hand as though it had touched fire. The soul was prompt to depart, eager to fly its frigid prison; there was only this shell to which honor might be done, only this emissary of his mother to which he could bring homage. He swore softly to himself that he would make this gesture, this insignificant repayment, swore it by the pinched, frightened aspect of the dead face in which he recognized himself. He would make the priests perform this—no matter what. It was little enough.

Across the gloomy hall he knocked on a door as dingy as the one he had just closed. When it opened, after a lengthy wait, the dimness within was barely distinguishable in the chink between door and frame, and the shadow which stood there a darker blur only.

"Mrs. Lally," he said—and thought, *these are the words that break death's bond of silence; I am coming back to life myself—.* "My mother's dead. Would you watch with her while I go . . . make arrangements?" The shadow moved a hand in the darkness and mumbled toothless prayers. "I'll be back," he said, and started down the stairs. "I'll be back."

The shadow moved into the lesser darkness of the hallway and showed gray-haired and bent. "Did you call the priest?" Mrs. Lally said.

Martin grunted. Always "the priest," he thought—as though there were only one, omnipotent and ubiquitous, constantly on the trail of death and need, arriving always in the nick of time. "I don't need the priest."

"I could call," Mrs. Lally said.

"I'll take care of things myself." He thrust himself down the creaking stairs, as a prayer started up from the old lips on the landing. "May her soul and all the souls of the faithful. . . ." Outside, the rain had begun again, scatteringly, as though there were a leak somewhere.

II

He rang the bell at the rectory defiantly and then stood in fear on the steps. Apprehension gnawed at his stomach and set up a tension in the organs that almost made him

15

tremble. It was a fear he was given to in the face of authority or power or even assurance. Even when Mr. Swanson spoke to him at the flower store, he experienced it. Now his anger waged a successful battle with it; he stomped around the top stone step in the hope that physical movement would relieve the tautness. He rang the bell again, digging his thumb deep against the metal button. Lights showed in the front windows off to his right; a dim hall-lamp lit the corridor through the curtained front door. But there was no response. It was as though they knew his mission and were determined to keep him outside where he was powerless. He rang a third time and received still no answer.

Nine o'clock . . . a bell bonged across the park. It was later than he thought—but not too late; not for the priests; they were always there, ready to serve, through snow and rain and sleet—like the mail service. He had gone endlessly up and down a path in the park, for how long he could not imagine—an hour, a lifetime—before he had been able to summon courage even to ring the bell, walking among the autumn ghosts of the trees, repeating again and again to himself the justice of his cause. A decent burial for his mother, some consideration besides the pauper's plot, squeezed in among the equally indigent dead; a fair measure of flowers; some slight pomp and ceremony out of the Church's deep reserve of ritual. He hoped he would encounter a priest other than Father Kirkman whom as an altar boy he had always feared. The priests would know his mother as one of the smug hollow faces at Wednesday Sodality, from her frequent, hungry appearances at the altar rail. They would know her as far as they could classify and distinguish among the monotonous countenances of the attentive, trusting poor. The figure of the shepherd and the flock was literal to the point of pain about the lambs; his mother had been one, bleating and obedient to the ancient deceptions. He knew better himself. He'd been around enough; he'd heard things. He knew the mock to which she gave her genuflection. His father had known, too. She was free of it now, anyway. But it wasn't free of her. The Church had a debt to pay.

Still there was no answer. He could come back later, but he mistrusted his own courage; its duration was doomed by the fickleness of emotion; he knew himself that well. The effort of will which had carried him up the steps might be difficult to achieve another time; now the anger was strong in him like lust. He peered in through the frosted glass, but there was only a vestibule and more doors beyond, and a shaded light. He would have to come back again. He would have to whip himself up again; the reasons were always there; the Church forbidding and admonishing, the priests restraining and commanding.

The steps curved away toward the sidewalk; from the third step down he had a better view of the lighted windows. He caught sight of a head and straining to his toes, the bulky, slumped body of old Father Kirkman, pacing toward the window. Martin raised his hand and shouted, but the figure did not see or hear. The old priest turned and padded away again, hands behind his back, disappearing below the sill as he moved toward the back of the room. He hadn't answered the bell. He was there and he hadn't answered. Anger waved in Martin's head, boldly and red. He remembered the coldness of his mother's cheek; the splintered floorboard and the peeling paint on the window sills. He remembered his father. And the bleakness of the corner of the cemetery where his father lay. He moved swiftly up the steps and tried the door. It was unlocked. The door in the vestibule was unlocked, as well. The door of the room where the priest walked was open. Martin stood in the doorway, panting, his heart beating louder than the priest's footfalls as the old man tramped toward the windows, hands behind his back, head bowed.

Martin could have turned back; could have gone out the doors and down the steps and across to the cool air of the park and the sigh of the October evening. He remembered this later. But the anger was like a rough towel close around his head, muffling out all except itself. Pitiable on the brass bed, his mother lay and was cold, and Mrs. Lally thumbed her beads in the gloom and there was only cold and dark and the promise of coldness and darkness forever. Amen.

"Father Kirkman," Martin said and heard himself shout. "Father Kirkman. You've got to do something about my mother."

The old man turned, blinking myopically through spectacles. Annoyance lit his face, the annoyance of a man who must add another burden, another intrusion to a life already infinitely badgered. He came toward Martin, the hands still behind his back, the shoulders stooped, peering at him. "Speak up, boy," the old priest said. "Speak up. Did you ring the bell?" He turned back toward the desk which stood before an old-fashioned fireplace, took a seat at it, not waiting for an answer. "I must have heard

18

you ringing—I thought it was—" A brass crucifix stood on the desk, obscuring Martin's view. "I'm sorry. Sit down. Sit down." The old priest coughed.

"I rang the bell. You didn't answer." Martin shouted again. What did this old man, this stupid old man know of death except as a routine matter; a later Mass on a weekday; a trip to a wind-blown hill to recite the worn-out prayers.

"My hearing," the old priest said. And coughed again. "We go all at once. The body runs down. The body knows." He craned around the crucifix. "You don't look well, boy. You're sick. Sit down."

Martin came up to the desk, leaned over the statue, shouted down. "My mother's dead. My mother's dead, do you hear? She died all alone with nobody there. You've got to give her a decent funeral. You've got to give her what she deserves."

"Dead." The old priest repeated the word tonelessly. "She's gone to her reward. She's out of it. What's your name, lad?"

"Lynn. Mrs. Martin Lynn, my mother was," Martin said, and found unaccountable tears ballooning in his eyes. And then proudly, "Mrs. Martin Lynn."

The old priest seemed to thumb through his mind as though among blurred index cards; he repeated the name over and over. "Martin Lynn . . . Martin Lynn. It sounds familiar."

The tears froze suddenly in Martin's eyes The anger blazed around him again, like lightning in his skull. "You're thinking of my father," he shouted again. "But that's all over. You can't remember that anymore. He's

19

gone for good. You saw to that. You can't bring him up again. But my mother died naturally—a good Catholic. And I want the best for her. I want a funeral fit for a millionaire. I want everything—all the trimmings. You've got to give it to me."

The old priest seemed to listen for the first time. He had a way of drawing his head back to one side and peering out of the corner of his eyes. "You're not sick," he said. "You're just angry. Don't be angry at death, my boy. It does no good."

In his eagerness and anger, Martin bumped the crucifix, almost tilted it to the floor; he caught it in time and set it right again. The old priest reached out to adjust it, centering his attention upon it. "She'll have the best, son," he said, straightening the brass figure. "She'll have the best."

"She better have," Martin breathed. "She better have."

"Sit down, boy," the old priest sighed and placed the palm of his hand wearily against his forehead. "Give me the name and address and all the rest of it. Couldn't you get to us before she died?"

Martin shook his head, saying nothing; he refused to move the conversation into friendly ground, refused to make contact across the blotter, the desk calendar, the brass crucifix, refused to be sucked in. The old priest poised a pen above a pad and wrote "Martin Lynn" heavily in a strong hand. Then looked up suddenly, "I remember your mother," he said. "A daily communicant. She was a devout woman. You should be grateful. Not all mourners have that consolation." Martin stared at him stubbornly, his breathing still heavy with his anger, his eyes burning. The priest rested his arm on the blotter, leaned over, peering around the crucifix. "But what's this about a big funeral?"

"I want my mother to go to her grave in . . . in triumph." He fished phrases out of dim literary recollections. "I want her to go with dignity. Not to be crammed into a casket and sneaked off when no one's looking. I want a lot of flowers, and a fine sermon to be preached, and a good plot of land. I want a decent funeral. Something . . . something to remember."

The old priest's gaze wandered. "Not that it matters," he said absently. "Not that it matters. The body puffs away underground. Mausoleums are for the living, boy. Not the dead. A lot they care. But . . . all this . . . it costs money."

Martin was on his feet again, his sleeve brushing the crucifix, tottering it. "You can do it. It isn't much to ask. You have money. You can fix it up with people. Mr. Swanson gives you all the flowers you want. I know; I deliver them. You can do this for my mother. You owe it to her."

The old priest looked pained. "Money . . . money," he murmured. "I can give you the sermon. Father Roth can preach you a sermon. But the rest of it takes money. Sit down, boy. It's a word we hate, you and I. But the body takes it seriously. What will it profit your mother? It isn't the flowers or where she lies that matters. I'll add her to my Mass."

"I want a big funeral, with flowers." The boy was tenacious, single-tracked, flushed. "I want a big funeral for my mother."

"You're overwrought, boy," the old priest said. "Don't

think I don't know. Death stays with you. You remember the dead ones. You give me your address and go along. I'll do the best I can. Everything'll be decent, don't you worry. A nice decent funeral."

"You said yourself she was good," Martin said, not shouting—dangerously not shouting. "You said yourself. You can't refuse this. You can't count out her goodness in coins."

The old priest looked around wearily, almost as though he was surprised to find himself in the old parish parlor. He had often dreamed of being out of it; many times in the past forty years he had imagined himself moving uptown to the Cathedral Parish and the fine, insolent house where the Bishop lived, wearing the red cape of the Monsignori and speaking at important dinners. There had been times he had come to hate the old gray parlor with its huge, vivid pictures. He had dreamed of leaving the room in triumph, in ascension. But here he had been, as young priest and old priest, for forty years—or was it more? At sixty-five, the past blended like distant earth and sky. Now his dream was only to leave the room behind, all the rooms, and go quietly into the hands of God; to avoid all such hotheaded young men as this one who now hovered over the crucifix; all men who shouted and gestured as though the issues of eternity could be wadded up into one moment which was worth all this perspiration. If there were only some way of relaying experience in its full impact; of telling young Martin Lynn, whose hair was damp on his forehead even in October (the boy looked familiar somehow; there were so many) that agitation was of no avail with God; that all moments of time, the humble and the harrowing, fitted somehow into a gigantic puzzle and one had only to wait with serenity to see how it worked out. If there were some way of stating the paradox of the material—that it was nothing and yet the only thing, valueless and priceless at the same time.

"You are out of your head with grief, my boy," the priest said, summoning pity out of his own store of suffering. "You must be resigned—as your mother was."

"I don't want pity," Martin said stormily. "That's all she got from you. A lot of good it did her. I don't want that."

But the quiet, beseeching word would do nothing, Father Kirkman knew; the soft answer increased wrath sometimes because it assumed superiority, left the foolish marooned high and ridiculous on the peak of their own folly and prompted retaliation. There was only sternness, decision; the faint echo of God's own magnificent wrath.

The priest's hand clapped loudly on the desk-top. "Don't talk like that!" The anger sounded genuine. "You haven't the money and that's an end of it." He lurched to his feet, stared imperially at the boy for a moment, then turned away toward the fireplace, presenting his broad, stooped back to the rage of Martin Lynn.

The boy stood lividly, blind anger twitching away at a corner of his mouth. The tension in his stomach which had begun as nervousness, tautened interminably, as though pulled by horses—and finally snapped. His right hand seemed to act with utter independence as it spread around the outstretched crossbar and the toppiece of the brass crucifix, raising it rapidly and decisively above his head.

"I want a big funeral." A kind of hopeless horror italicized the words and he lunged at the priest and brought the base of the figurine down devastatingly on the old, worried skull. It made a plushy sound as though he had punched a pillow.

After the thump—a surprisingly light, collapsing thump —of the black-cassocked body on the hearth, there was no sound for a long time. It was quieter even than the vigil Martin had kept beside his mother. No cars passed in the street; no rain peppered the windows; no one coughed. The old priest was unbelievably silent; his spectacles, intact, dangled grotesquely from one ear; except for the distorted position of one arm, he appeared at rest, as though he had lain down in the middle of the room for a rather unconventional nap. Martin stared down at him, his mouth open, his eyes blank—his anger vanished magically by one sweep of his arm. In one swift gesture the resentment of a young lifetime was dispersed; this was a hypnotism he had never heard of. But it was over now and the old priest could get up; they could finish their conversation. They had been talking about . . . something. . . .

The brass figurine throbbed in his hand. Stiffly, he brought it up within range of his vision; fresh, curiously-red blood clung about the head, dripped thinly along the side of the corpus, as though delicately spaded on by a frugal artist; just enough to give the illusion that the body on the Cross was bleeding, just a very little bit commensurate with the miniature scale. He flung it from him spasmodically; it clanged against the red bricks of the fireplace and plummeted to the hearth beside the priest's feet. The noise acted like a signal; a pealing of bells was set off suddenly in the boy's head, metallic and relentless, ringing on and on, and he had covered his ears with his hands and looked beseechingly about him, saying "O God! O God!" before he realized that it was the doorbell—the doorbell—the doorbell buzzing through the empty house as it had done for him a short while before.

Collapse succeeded panic. He dropped to his knees beside the desk, buried his head in his hands and waited, trying to pray, his lips fumbling and quivering among the forgotten words, piecing out an appeal for mercy. "Hail Mary, full of grace . . . hallowed be thy name . . . on earth as it is in heaven . . . O my God, I am heartily sorry." He wondered how he would explain this horrible dream to his mother when morning filtered in among the fire escapes and lowered at the smudged windowpanes.

He was aware that the ringing had stopped; as a sound sometimes reaches the consciousness minutes after its occurrence, so the silence, the lack of the bell's high-pitched insistence, struck him belatedly. A shuffling on the stone steps indicated that some less persistent visitor had abandoned the bell, had gone down the steps and away—a blessed journey he himself might have taken earlier. It was the only time in his life that he wished his cowardice had conquered; tonight, of all times, he must push on, must keep his word to himself; tonight he had been brave. He gasped deeply as a new onslaught of tears threatened him. And then it occurred to him: no one had answered the bell; no one had seen him come; no one knew he was here. Why couldn't he leave, quietly, stealthily—follow those retreating footsteps down to the street, take his place unobtrusively in the night along with all the hundreds of others who looked no different than he? This was all a terrible mistake in any case—a ridiculous, unreasonable error unconnected with anything in his life that had gone before it. He could go out now, go home through the cool brown October evening and read tomorrow in the paper about the old priest's death (for he had no doubt of death) and ask himself with justice as he read the staccato, stereotyped accounts: Who has done this thing?

The action decided upon, he moved with swiftness. The old priest lay still in the wry position he had taken up to accommodate death. He had fallen over head first toward the fireplace in such a way that the wound on his head was not visible to Martin. It was as though he had stumbled and would arise at any moment. Martin placed an inexpert hand among the bunched folds of the cassock but could find no evidence of a beating heart. He arose, looked quickly around the room; there was nothing to reveal his presence. He must get out as quickly as he could. But first he must check obvious evidence of his visit. He moved around behind the desk, stepping carefully over the old priest's body, stood beside the chair. The blotter was in place, the inkwell, the pad—he noticed his name where the priest had written in a shimmering scrawl. He ripped the page from the pad and pocketed it. For the first time he noticed, poked under the leather rim of the blotter, a photograph. It was the picture of a girl in First Communion dress, faded somewhat with the passage of years, a girl bright with innocence and expectancy, the young face crinkled in a smile, the wide-apart eyes open with the joy of an occasion. He absorbed an impression from it at a glance and had an instantaneous feeling that there was a resemblance to the face of the old priest. There was nothing else; he had no hat. He started toward the door. Everything then was in place except the crucifix and that he need not touch; the reason for its movement would be obvious. There was no link with him. Except possibly . . . fingerprints?

From the doorway he turned back into the room. The desk blocked his vision; from where he stood there was neither priest nor crucifix visible. His physical memory asserted itself and for a moment he felt as though he were entering the room for the first time; that there was nobody there; that he had come in vain. And a breath of relief swept over him, only to become a chill of terror as a more powerful memory blanketed his bones with revulsion. He recrossed the room, circling the desk from the opposite side this time, away from the corpse. The crucifix lay where he had thrown it, face down on the hearth, a tinge of blood on the bricks beneath it.

He felt the sweat break out tangibly on his forehead as he stooped to pick it up. His fingers touched the blood and he was conscious of a mingled sensation of stickiness and cold. Grasping it by the top—where he had held it before—he set it upright on the desk, took out his handkerchief and sponged away at the head, the shoulders, the upright where it projected above the daintily tilted head. Blood smeared onto his handkerchief. He had no idea how vigorously fingerprints must be rubbed to be erased. He suspected, however, that brass might delineate them rather clearly and he took special pains to rub it soundly . . . rubbing away at the blood on Christ's head, plunging his handkerchief among the thorns, removing evidence from a place where, in a sense, it was not removable, not ever. The thought struck a new chill into him; so that he caught his breath convulsively and ran from the room, out into the corridor, through the doors, banging them behind him so that their glass panels rattled. He came to a halt halfway down the stone steps outside, leaning against the balustrade breathlessly. The handkerchief was still in his hand and he stuffed it clumsily into the pocket of his coat. A shiver passed over him from the cool night air and he felt the perspiration on his forehead dry coldly against the breeze. Slowly he descended to the street, his hands held stiffly at his sides, his head frozen erect, his breath issuing heavily from his throat. He had an inexplicable impulse to scream, but it passed almost before he was conscious of it. "Hail Mary, full of grace," he found himself praying again, again unaccountably, and remembered, for no reason he could assign, that a garish painting of the Immaculate Conception hung over the fireplace in the rectory—a detail he had not been consciously aware of before—hung now over the stained crucifix and the inert body of old Father Kirkman. ". . . the Lord is with thee, blessed art thou among women. . . ."

It came to him with the shock of news, like a headline in a morning paper, that his mother was dead. He couldn't remember when he had forgotten it.

III

The girl sat sullenly far over in the seat of the car away from the driver. She was entirely motionless. Where before, at the beginning of the drive back to town, her hands had worked and twisted against one another and she had cast dark looks at her companion, now she sat listlessly, staring unseeingly at the screen of the car window on which the travelog of the fleeing countryside unreeled itself. The grind of the motor, the white rug of road running steadily beneath them, the flicker of lights in the square shapes of houses, which now became more frequent, had triumphed over the jerky rhythm of her scattered emotions and quieted her. She pointedly avoided looking at the driver, gave no sign at all that she was aware of his presence; the car might have been steering itself, drawn by the magic glare of its own headlights along the sweep of night.

The man turned toward her, the strained young face and Roman collar visible in the light from the dashboard. "It's a closed incident, of course," he said. "No one need ever know." She didn't look at him, didn't even pay the negative courtesy of concentrating obviously on the window. She just sat. "I wanted you to know that," he said. "It's forgotten."

"It's not a closed incident for me," she said, and closed that incident, decisively.

"If it's still open, then that's better." It was as though her speech had provided an opening, into which he tried to pry the wedge of further persuasion. "The other way, it would have been closed, definitely and for good. This way you have—what? Another chance, perhaps. People have offered their souls for that."

She was stubbornly silent. They passed a car going in the opposite direction, its lights bobbing over the scowl and pout of her face which was autumnal itself under the autumn hat, behind the symmetrical cosmetics. The lights and the opposing whir of the other motor hurtled past and the car dug lonesomely over the road again. Street lights dotted the blackness now; they passed a service station; an all-night restaurant. The proximity of other people threatened her reserve of silence.

"Will he never leave me alone?" she burst out. "Since I was a girl, following me around as though I were moronic. I'm grown now. I'm a woman." She looked straight ahead, venting her anger on the periphery of the light-glow ahead.

"Should he stop loving you for that?" the young priest asked.

"Love!" the girl said. "What does he know about that? Sending you after me to interfere with love. I love Malcolm. I know."

"If it's love, it'll wait," the young priest said. "The edge of doom. Love knows how to wait better than anything." He wished there were stronger words, words that would fit into the buzzing car and the dim light, words that would carry across the three feet of leather and penetrate the smartly-groomed head, the neat hat, the anger. But they were almost there now and he had done nothing, said nothing, except impetuous, stubborn things which had antagonized her. He wondered now how he had had the brazenness to carry the scene through; he had made no friends for the Church tonight. He remembered the Justice of the Peace in his neatly-pressed trousers and crumpled shirt saying "Here, here. What's going on?" He remembered the Justice's wife in the doorway, stern and

30

indifferent, against a glow of candles on a cake (provided for a slight extra charge). He remembered Malcolm, the handsome, thwarted groom, incredulous and urbane at first, then protesting vituperatively. And the girl, humiliated above all, stung and embarrassed because she recognized the partial validity of the claim he presented in behalf of the old priest, who was her uncle. In the end she had been persuaded by her shame, bitterly turning away and rushing out to his car as the bubble burst, as the occasion was irrevocably ruined, as the dream was soiled and pawed by clumsy, obtuse hands. Only a fierce and unaccustomed determination had enabled the young priest to bring off the incident at all; his own embarrassment burned in his cheeks; and it was hardly a triumph. Resentment hung tangibly on the air as he left the house and drove the car away, past the double-faced highway sign on which the lettering "Justice of the Peace" referred now to the seething old man behind him who had closed the book.

"I'm glad you came," he had told the girl.

"How could I face Malcolm now," she had said and had assumed thereafter her silence—as an insult to him.

There would be a time, the young priest thought, when he might brag of this. I prevented a civil marriage, he might say. It would sound heroic and shining, the valorous deed of the Defender of the Faith. But in the moment itself, he had felt only shame. The thwarting of a will bent, in whatever direction, had about it the atmosphere of usurpation, of tyranny: a meddling in God's Providence. He had suggested this to the old priest earlier in the evening, but to no avail. "She's my niece," the old man had said stubbornly across the desk, his eyes riveted on the crucifix which had been given him at ordination. "I know her better than she knows herself. It's the best thing." And the young priest had set out on his distasteful journey, praying for its rightness as much as for its success. There had been, of course, no compulsion to go; he had returned from administering the Last Sacraments to find the old man fuming and worrying in the parlor about his wayward niece, and had accepted the charge out of his affection for his superior, who could not manage the errand himself.

They were at the rectory door now. A light burned in the parlor, though it was after midnight.

"I won't go in," the girl said, still looking straight ahead, her hands composed in her lap, her head obscured in shadows, a bracelet only showing signs of life in the gloom. "I don't want to see him."

"Just for a moment," the young priest said. "After all, I am only his messenger. You owe him that."

"I owe him nothing," she said, the voice stony and toneless.

"He only did it out of love," the young priest insisted. "Try to realize that. Love uses strange forms. He considers you—almost a daughter."

"I would say he's not quite a father," the girl replied bitterly. "It's only his selfishness. He's hanging on to me; he's afraid I'll wake up, grow up, recognize his . . . prejudices."

"Not selfishness," the young priest said. "You ought not say that. Do you think this thing was easy for him. He would rather die than tell me about it even. It was shameful to him. Yet he did. And he did not send me in obedience; it was a request; a plea, rather. Personal."

"You too are a martyr, I suppose?"

"I would do anything for him. That's all."

"So much love," the girl said, "and not one marriage. Not one for me."

"If you are so positive you are right, that he is wrong, then have at least the courage to tell him so."

"I'll tell him," she said, and the anger partook partly of the tone of a sob. She had not wept all evening; all the dryness and hotness at the corner of her eyes had been resentment. Now it was melting down: as she climbed from the car, crossed the sidewalk and ran up the curved stone steps. Her anger spelled itself out into hot words across her brain; she composed defiance upon defiance to fling into the old man's face: the heels clattered, the bracelet jangled, the tears came. She flung open the door, the withering words eager and sharp on her lips.

The young priest closed the car door and watched her go, breathing silent prayers that this procedure had been the wise, the prudent one. That the evening would not beget a hatred and bitterness which would put her forever beyond the pale of the serene. He determined to go quietly along the corridor to his own room, past the family quarrel, the invective, the reproof, the petty battle of affections. He gained the foot of the stairs and then, of course, he was recalled by her scream.

IV

Martin wondered, unable to decide what to do with his hands. He still carried them stiffly at his sides, like valises, foreign burdens he must bear which had no connection with him. In his pockets, they were leaden; they seemed to chill his face as he passed them over his cheeks. He carried them over street after street, managing them with difficulty over the intersections, where they felt naked, more exposed. Up curb and down curb, along the smooth, lined sidewalks he went, not daring to stop and rest.

Gradually the tumbled, taut chaos of his mind was shaken down into some kind of examinable order. "I had not meant—I had not meant—I had not meant——" he tried to tell himself, but even the thought perished and died under the vigorous life of other, accusing memories. Even the strange grisliness of his hands could not wring repentance from him. He *had* meant. The blow had been a savage answer to so many refusals: the standard commandments of the catechism, the soft don'ts of his mother, the cursory, repetitious denials of the confessional where virtue signaled warmly in the dark; the negations in the fat form of Father Kirkman, shuffling in to don his vestments for early Mass, as another altar boy and Martin placed the wine and lit the candles. The jeweled affluence of the Church and the paltriness of his mother's apartment had created an inexplicable division in him as long ago as he could remember. The splendor and the sordidity side by side; the gleam of the monstrance and the crestfallen poor box; the glittering symbols on the chasuble and the tatter of the congregation. And always the no's

34

and the reminders; the suffering in silence; the daily cross which is yours to cherish. And this final, irreparable paradox: his mother's devotion and the priest's refusal. Everybody knew the Catholic Church had ways of doing things; there were methods. It wasn't what you knew, but who—. He beat his hands desperately against his sides. The scene repeated itself before his eyes, like the second showing of a movie; and all the details were the same; all his hot emotions identical; the same movements: the grip on the brass crucifix, the lunge forward, the crushing downward blow; and then the amazement. He would have liked to stop the film, to change the details: something other than the crucifix to hold in the hand. But it wound off inexorably; the projector had the hum of fate, going on and on. The film was made now; the picture complete, even down to the last reel, which he could not see. The Church stood as before; rich and impregnable; he walked the streets, without money, without hope. And the greatest of these——?

At a street corner, a car swung perilously close to him, honking. He was too sluggish to move quickly; it swept close to him, the tires plushing on the asphalt, turned the corner and vaulted away. His eyes followed it: a police squad car. The idea of official investigation occurred to him tangibly for the first time. He had erased the fingerprints, torn the pad to conceal his deed from—whom? the painting on the wall? A shadow? The confessional? It was an imitative act, automatic once he had accepted the tag of criminal. The accusers, blue-coated, brass-buttoned, writing stolidly in notebooks, were a new vision for him. Their similarity to the Church's respresentatives struck him suddenly: they were inevitable, slow-footed, sure and relentless. It must be close to midnight or close to—he had no idea. How long had he walked? Tiredness clamped on the calves of his legs. Had they discovered the old man yet? Were other feet padding around the desk, prying among the writing things, searching among the folds of the cassock for the beat of a heart which had stopped?

A neon light drew him into a diner where he ordered coffee and looked with stunned curiosity at the strange figure reflected in the mirror behind the counter. His hair was mussed, almost matted; his eyes glared; there was a smudge along the corner of his mouth. His hands reached toward the corner of his lips; the mark was dry, solid. He pried it off with his fingernails and looked dumbly at its dark-brown color. He remembered the stained handkerchief then and the sheet of paper with his name on it he had snatched from the pad. He had not disposed of them. He reached into his pocket and found them there. He could have dropped them anywhere along the street during his walk: let the wind catch them along a curb, down a sewer. But they were there crumpled and wadded in his pocket.

Two men entered the diner, sat down beside him, as the attendant brought his coffee. They were burly, assured-looking; they sat and said nothing, holding menu cards in beefy hands.

"Is there a men's room?" Martin asked the man behind the counter. The man pointed. "The little door at the end." Martin slid off the stool and started past the men, his hand going nervously to the handkerchief, gripping it.

He would stuff it into a wastebasket or flush it down—relief swept over him.

"Wait a minute, buddy." The second of the two men swung round on his stool, put a restraining hand on Martin's arm. The grip was firm, not a casual touch; panic nibbled at him. The man turned his face toward the attendant. "Is there any other exit in there?" he asked.

"Not unless you're a water-rat," the attendant grinned out from under the cocked white cap. "There ain't no door, Mac."

"Okay," the man said, but the hand stayed firm, like iron. His head swung back to Martin. "We want to talk to you, buddy."

It was clear to him suddenly that they were policemen; the felt hats pulled low, the immobile faces, the big hands and the broad shoulders. He blurted before he could stop himself: "I haven't done anything. I'm on my way home."

The men exchanged glances. "What gave you that idea?" the first one said. "Who said you'd done anything?"

How did you act unsuspicious, Martin wondered. He would have said the same thing under any circumstances to a policeman. But he had made his error in guessing their identity; it was an epilogue to guilt. But an innocent man might have done that, he thought; the innocent were the most afraid; they had their crimes ahead of them; the spectre of the future. He concentrated on controlling his voice so it would not tremble. "What do you want?"

"Did you enjoy the movie?" the second asked him.

"Yeah, how was it?" the first one added.

"How about the part where the gangster traps the girl on the building?" the first one said.

"—And she pushed him over. How about that?"

"I haven't been to a movie." The screen in his mind began to unroll the scene in the rectory; the old priest turned toward the fireplace—himself gripping the figurine. "I haven't been to a movie for a long time."

"We saw you at the Galaxy tonight," the first man said.

"With a girl," the second one added quickly. Their questions came fast, like sharp blows.

"I wasn't with a girl," Martin said. "Not tonight." He could see the small intense man in the army office, peering over the pencil. No sexual experience, the man had said. He was a psychiatrist. None at all. That's bad, boy—bad.

"But you were at the Galaxy?" the first man asked, leaning down from the stool. "You were there."

"I wasn't," Martin said. "I wasn't. How could I go to a movie after what happened today. How could I?"

"What happened today?" the second man caught him up swiftly. He could see the two faces now, like balloons, slanted together, questioning at him.

He screamed at them: "My mother died, that's what happened. My mother died." He broke from the momentarily relaxed grip and fled for the small door, banged it with his hand and was through. He heard them shouting as he stuffed the handkerchief into a tall wire basket, already overflowing with soggy paper towels. There was no time to do more. The door flapped open and the first man stood in the opening: a hand on the door, a hand on the frame, eyeing him. Martin stood still, his head lowered.

"Listen, buddy," the man said, not moving, "if you're on

the level, nothing will happen to you. We're detective bureau." A badge flashed. "But we're working on a robbery. Somebody held up the cashier at the Galaxy, shot her and got a couple thousand dollars. We'll have to look you over."

Martin trembled beside the wastebasket. The slip of paper was in his pocket; he fancied he could see the bloody handkerchief glowing among the discarded towels. "I've nothing to be ashamed of," Martin said, near to sobbing. "I just want to be let alone."

The man came behind him. "No use running. The door's blocked." His heavy hands slapped up and down Martin's back, fingered agilely into the pockets, extracting things: the slip of paper, some small change, the thin wallet, two keys, a rosary (no longer would his mother insist that he carry that).

"You Martin Lynn?" the man was reading the priest's handwriting. Dead men tell no tales, thought Martin. He nodded. "Why'd you write your name?"

He told the truth. "I was arranging about the funeral," he said, and felt genuine tears in his eyes. His mother was dead. She would still be lying on the bed, colder and colder in the gloom; Mrs. Lally would be gone by now. There would be only the darkness and the cold and the motionless form, face upward on the bed, stiff and chill.

The man slapped open the wallet, riffled the picture of his mother, his driver's permit, the celluloid calendar, the draft card. "You won't have to carry that any longer," he said. Martin reddened; his wallet was full of information; the private secret sprung open in a number and a dash and a letter. The man returned everything to him.

"We'll want your name," the man said. "We'll see you when you come out." The door flapped shut and Martin was alone. A huge sob racked him; it was as though he could regurgitate his sorrow, his pain, his sin. He stuffed the things into his pocket; all except the paper; that he tore into pieces and dropped into one of the bowls. He retrieved the handkerchief from the wire basket, digging deep among the loose pile of towels. He threw it after the bits of paper, engulfed both of them in the sucking, chortling water. They were gone, at any rate. All the evidence outside him was invisible now; only the haunting prints on the soul remained and they were not material for the police.

The irony of their questioning struck him then. A woman shot, money stolen; and they suspected him. Somewhere along his system there was a sardonic laugh but it could not fight its way among the twisted nerves, the unmalleable muscles, the tautened soul—to his lips. He was being accused of—the wrong crime. As for shooting, even the army hadn't wanted him for that. Hysteria rattled in his throat, threatened to force him to shout. He bent over a wash basin, grasping the faucets in his hands, in a silent, strangling convulsion. He was spinning round and round with his mother and they were laughing, laughing; the room was a blur; his thoughts tangled, red and blue and a revolving purple. And then he was sick, liquidly and sourly, and the room settled down again: the streaked white basin, the dark walls with the exposed pipes, the shuttered stalls, the enameled trough. He straightened up unsteadily, his head reeling. When he reached for his handkerchief, he remembered, and plucked paper towels out of the metal container instead. If he could only stop thinking, he murmured to himself as he sponged his face. If he could only function mechanically for awhile until the whirl of questions and the indistinguishable pulp of events could take shape in his mind. He was beginning to lose track even of the sequence now. He told himself he was standing in a washroom and two detectives waited outside the thin, narrow door and his coffee was getting cold. The picture of the coffee cup revived him. He could drink it while he gave them his name and address; it would help to compose him. It would occupy his hands. As he opened the door, he found himself praying, in the same garbled way as before. From a Friday afternoon catechism class he remembered the face of Father Kirkman: "Prayer is in the intention, not the form," the old priest had said, sniffling away at a head cold. Martin was grateful the words were not all.

The two men did not look up as he passed them on the way to his stool. Only the white-capped attendant followed him with surprised eyes; even with respect, Martin thought. He was an object of interest now. Wanted by the police. Five feet eight inches tall, one hundred forty pounds, formerly employed as truck driver—he took his seat, confidently, almost proudly. The detectives looked up from twin pieces of pie; their similarity went to great lengths. They were kindly now. When he gave them his address and age, one of them noted it down in a leather-covered book.

"Sorry about your mother, Lynn," the second one said, "but we got a job. You look suspicious."

"We may still want to see you again," the other warned.

He wondered if he dared ask the question which lurked on his tongue. It seemed natural enough to him. He could feel the attendant's eyes on him and decided to chance it.

"Was this—" the coffee helped to moisten his throat, to relax his stomach. "Was this cashier . . . killed?"

"We don't know—yet," the second man answered him.

"Why?" the first one demanded with a touch of his former gruffness.

"I—I—just wondered," Martin mumbled. He had wondered—what? How the guilt compared; whether the gunman who wandered somewhere outside the circle of the diner's neon light bore a blacker weight than his; whether he was being accused of more or less than was his just due? If he were arrested for the robbery: he could always say, I didn't do it. I couldn't have done it. I was busy at the time. Doing what? Oh, smashing an old priest over the head with a crucifix. Yes, I couldn't have done it. I was sinning elsewhere.

The detectives finished their pie. "We may be around to look you up," one of them said. "We may be around later." They paid their bill and moved heavily to the door.

He drank his coffee slowly, listening to their footsteps clacking on the pavement outside. He watched their bulky figures disappear into the side of the mirror opposite the counter, moving off-screen, out of the picture for the moment.

The attendant was beside him, leaning down, elbows on the counter, white cap tilted over precariously. "Those cops," the attendant said. "What they won't do. It's a wonder they didn't question me. I was at the Galaxy last night. But they had the story all fouled up. She didn't push him; he pushed her."

"Yeah?" Martin said. He thought he would like to stay here in the diner, drinking coffee, among the smell of onions and the mist from the coffee urn. It was familiar and inoffensive and even—yes, comforting. The counterman, who was thin and freckled and red-haired, spoke to him decently, equally. He knew when he went out into the street again he would see the old priest and the crucifix and the painting of the Immaculate Conception and the blood. And his mother. The film winding on and on. Continuous performance. Comfortable seats. Smoking in the loges. Once the deed was recorded, once the film printed, there was no recourse. "Cut" they said on the movie lots. "Print it!" they said, and the glass heroines were recorded forever on a strip of celluloid. None of the gestures could be redone, none of the positions altered, none of the actions changed. It was that much like life.

The counterman was occupied still with the motion picture. "Only she didn't fall when he pushed her. She couldn't fall. It was Rita Hayworth."

The immunity of the chosen, thought Martin. Always the hero emerged triumphantly in the final reel, surviving securely against whatever insuperable odds, preserved by convention. Always the hero, breathless on the screen, and you, breathless in the seat, safe from harm—the bullet averted, the collision missed, the love faithful. It was the way the rich were protected in life, with the happy ending guaranteed on the society pages. Almost never did the unhappy fate overtake; the eye had time to be dry when the lights went up.

The horror of the evening began to rehearse itself once more in his mind. The old priest shaking his head wearily, the bell buzzing through the rectory endlessly, ringing on and on until it seemed to attack his ear again, and the blood flowing, flowing, creeping daintily down the brass ribs. He threw a coin on the counter and left the diner. He had said he was going home. He would go home, then —wherever it was.

V

He found the door open and the flat entirely dark. It was after one o'clock. Of course, Mrs. Lally had long since hobbled back to her bed, mumbling her prayers across the dim hall, streaming Hail Marys from gloomy door to gloomy door. He pushed the door in and stood in fear on the threshold. The idea of the body abandoned and alone on the brass bed struck out of the darkness at him accusingly. He had gone abruptly off in search of peace for her and brought back to the cold corpse only additional pain. He wondered if he could add depth to the lines in her forehead even in death, or more strain still to the thin lips. There was no one to worry about him now; no one to lament his lostness or pray over his despair. His comfort had become his fear and he dreaded to approach the hands which would no longer soothe, the fingers stiff and stretched and cemented into a position.

He stood at the door staring into the darkness until he began to doubt that he would ever see again. But as soon as he did, shapes began to appear. Death itself grinned evilly out of the gloom, glinting white in the blackness. In a frenzy he stepped inside the door and switched on the light, his fingers scratching against the metal plate which contained the buttons.

The light sprang up on a cheap print framed in discolored wood on the wall. The same vacuous face cast heavenward, the serpent conquered, the fat cherubim suspended round the triumph. It was a smaller reproduction of the same Immaculate Conception that fluttered over the still figure of the old priest. He let out a cry, smothering it with his hand as it choked in the quiet room. He leaned against the wall moaning softly to himself. The clues, he thought. He had obliterated the ones which he had left behind; but the trail scattered beforehand, the bread crumbs sieved through the hand on the way toward the fatal rendezvous, these would require a lifetime of picking up. The footprints of the return could not wholly obscure the marks of the approach. The signs would be everywhere, like personal hieroglyphics, decipherable only to himself. Handkerchiefs and pieces of paper were irrelevant; the real clues were embedded in ineradicable places not to be drifted down with a flash and gurgle of water.

He flung himself through the drapes, groped blindly toward the bed, hungry even for the shell of consolation. "Mother. Mother." He sighed gratingly, hollowly into the gloom, doubting death itself for a moment, hoping for a movement from the frail form. He fell on his knees. In the change from the light of the other room, nothing was visible to him. His hands found the mattress, the cheap cover paper-thin to his search, searched and fumbled over the uneven, inflexible surface of the bed. Far in each direction his hands stretched frantically, pleading even the unnaturally cold body. But there was nothing there. The bed was empty even of the cadaver.

She was gone. Not even the coldest comfort of all remained.

He dropped his head on his hands and began to weep in the dimness, the tension, the disappointment, the despair seeping out from him in a whimper. He cried without restraint, all the horror and shock of the day pressing him in iron arms; his body the limp avenue of his soul's distraction. He was the instrument of his own torture.

There was a sound behind him then; a footfall? a skirt's rustle? a hand on the doorknob? He turned quickly in spasmodic response to his terror, seated on the floor now, the back of his head knocking against the brass footpiece. A shadow was outlined in the doorway: old, bent, black, female. His mother resurrected in the gloom! Come back to stand as always, unchanging, forgiving; to disperse the cloud of dream he had labored under. "I knew it couldn't have happened. It was all so silly," he said to her. "I thought I was a murderer." He could have laughed.

But the figure spoke. Not in the gray, faded accents of his mother—the sweetness which contained hope in the face of all hopelessness—but in an older, quivering crackle. "Poor boy." The figure said. "Poor boy." And it was only old Mrs. Lally after all, and reality blinded him again, striking down at him with the force of lightning, setting the machine in his head awhir again, driving at him again and again with hammer-strokes of dreadful fact. "Poor boy!" said Mrs. Lally. And he found himself in a kind of peace, which was numbness. He could no longer feel the chill of the brass against the nape of his neck or the fatigue

in his legs or the constriction in his throat. He was here
only in this half-lit room with an old woman, who was
speaking to him. The voice came as on a clear summer day
across a broad field devoid of wind, of breath. As though
the air itself was sucked out of the universe and everything hung in a haze of anesthesia.

"The priest came soon after you left," she was saying in
this dry, barren climate, this vacuum. "He was too late,
of course, for anything but a conditional ceremony, the
Lord rest her soul. But he called the funeral home from
the phone at the foot of the stairs and I signed the papers
and they took her away, the Lord rest her soul. They were
here within the hour. I waited up for you. You mustn't
worry now. The blessings do come after all. God doesn't
forget."

The voice trailed away into repetitions. The clouds of
reality drifted down through the clear, vacant universe.
Her voice chanted on as though exorcising this precious
vacuity, this friendly nothingness. Color crept back into
the light, his lungs fluttered again with the gusts of life.

"To Murray's they took her. A fine Catholic man. And
expensive, too. The priest said he'd arrange about the
money, whatever it was. Mr. Murray was always most
obliging. They have fine parlors there and always a sweet
smell of the flowers. You'd think it was a garden itself. The
blessings do come, praise the Lord."

He tried to single out the blessings. Father Kirkman had
been murdered. His anger had climbed up and rattled the
gates of heaven. He had wiped blood from a crucifix. The
blessings did come.

"You must sleep now," Mrs. Lally said, imitating the

forgotten tones of a mother. "There's nothing to be done till tomorrow. You must sleep and pray, pray and sleep, as the Lord wills. This day is over and you can be thankful it is. Tomorrow's another one."

She was beside him, helping him to his feet. He swayed and had to hold the bed for support. She murmured and cooed all the while she led him back to the outer room, to the couch where he had habitually slept. He staggered and almost fell once. But finally he was there, stretching awkwardly out on the rough coverlet, the one his mother had always removed and replaced with sheets for him. He hadn't slept well for a long time now, not since his father's death. He wondered if he would sleep now. But she was speaking, mumbling words like dim flashes of light in a dense night. He tried to see them, to make out the design. Something about her staying beside him. Something about a cup of tea. The familiar phrase was a comfort briefly and deceptively. He tried to bring it into focus but it sped out of his vision like the dot always beyond the scope of the astigmatic eye.

He shook his head, tried to tell her to leave him, and she must have heard, for a while later he was lying on the couch and he was alone in the room and he thought he would go to sleep after all since there was nothing to be done until morning and the blessings did appear after all. In disguises, he thought, turning his head toward the wall, spiraling his tense, exhausted body, seeking the comfortable position. But there was no posture of ease on the lumpy couch, no arrangement against which the muscles did not cramp and complain. He hoped that across the hall Mrs. Lally was praying for him, forming the old shapes of words clearly among her broken teeth; praying that he would sleep; that he would rest in peace. But he did not sleep. And then he heard a floorboard creak and was aware, even in the blanketing darkness, that the door was opening.

VI

The girl sat on a stiff chair in the corridor and tried to cry, hoping for tears to streak the carefully-planned face. Off somewhere she could hear the young priest's voice, high and precise, attempting coherence as he talked to the police. She had watched him give conditional absolution to the old man. "The second time tonight," he told her vaguely and repeated the prayers fervently. She had been given to racking shudders ever since she had seen the body, a coldness that ran along her body tangibly and shook her as though she were a doll. She had not seen his face: she could recall only a heap of black and a smear of red and the noncommittal, casual black shoes protruding awkwardly side by side, one on top of and slightly advanced from the other. She had screamed and the young priest had led her out of the room to this chair and she had only sat, inertly, except for the occasional chill.

"If you do this," Father Kirkman had told her once, severely, across the desk inside, "it will kill your mother." The deed had been some insignificant ambition of adolescence; a weekend trip, a notorious friend, something now forgotten. She had probably done it in any case. Now she had attempted another forbidden excursion and he himself lay dead, violently behind the desk. The connection presented itself: she had wished him dead often enough. The stocky, fattening old man with the full gray hair had stood year after year as a barrier to her maturity; persuading, pleading, commanding, repeating the same precepts in the same words, confident that reiteration was enough. Her chains were broken now and she should have been glad but regret lurked somewhere under the assured hat, regret at least if not a sorrow that could speak in tears. Her decisions would be all her own henceforth; no longer would this gray-haired guardian angel stake out the signposts, pointing the direction virtue led so that she might stubbornly choose the dangerous path. Now, for instance, she and Malcolm might be married as they chose, whenever, at whatever place, in whatever unsacramental slattern white house set back carefully from the unfrequented road. She might have left the girl Rita Conroy behind forever, with all her little Catholic tricks. It occurred to her she might be married this minute, exulting in the flesh while her uncle's corpulent body sprawled in quite a different attitude upon the bloody hearth. The thought coincided with a tremble, the body shaking off the unwelcome, shattering vision of the old man slain, like a dog ridding himself of water after a dip.

The young priest came out of the death-room where he had been telephoning. "It looks," he said drearily, "as though he'd been hit on the head," and waited, as though the incomprehensible idea might penetrate his brain, open the door and fit in among the orderly concepts, the faith and the hope.

"The police?" she asked, not looking at him. She was conscious, suddenly, that this man knew so much of her;

to know even the last four hours was revelation enough. Almost as though he had heard her confession, babbling the bare events, strained of motivations, through the grill.

"They're on the way," he said. Then, "You'd better go."

"But—" she began. A vague loyalty suggested that she stay; she had assumed she would remain.

"There's nothing you can do," he said. "I'll tell them you were here. Whatever else there is to tell. There's no relation between you and this." He gestured toward the door behind him. "There's no reason why the police should know your——"

She guessed that he would have said "shame"; the Catholic vocabulary maintaining its traditional meanings, its musty connotations even in crisis. "He would have preferred that, I'm sure," the young priest added. "I'll get in touch with you tomorrow."

"I don't care if they know," she told him, defiance echoing clumsily along the hall, breaking invisibly over the desk and the cold body.

"He would have cared," the young priest said simply. "He was worried about your good name as well as your soul. Besides, it would reflect on him; now in the hour of his death."

She knew then that his concern was for the dead man rather than for her and plugged a sudden hole of disappointment with the conclusion that that was natural enough surely. No one would fret about her now from the same curious, cautionary standpoint, measuring her defiant feminine movements against an eternal yardstick.

"I will not withhold information," he assured her. "If it must come out, it must come out. But since it is not actually relevant. . . ." His voice trailed away. "Struck on the head," he said, and seemed to shudder himself; whether his lips moved in tremor or in prayer she could not be sure.

He opened the door for her. "Pray for him," the young priest said. Their earlier relationship as opponents had rearranged itself quietly into a formality born of their proximity and share in the old man; death had intervened to stop the war, to call a truce.

She envisioned her prayers, shy and undernourished, pleading skinnily at the throne of God. She nodded, saying nothing, and went down the stone steps, her heels chipping away at the worn stones. It was the first time she had descended these steps without anger, without inarticulate plans for revenge. The rain had stopped and the moon poked palely among the clouds. Well, the revenge was accomplished now. She was free—a woman.

VII

Moonlight found its way with difficulty into the room, the blank wall of the building outside the windows halting just low enough so that a patch was permitted to fall into the room at certain hours of the night, in the early morning, just about now. The patch was pale and almost rectangular now on the door, tipping the round knob, spraying delicately on the scratched lock and the marred wood. It was dim, ghostly, hardly a light at all. But in its nebulous area the knob turned slowly, the latch clicked, the door swung in.

He had always been afraid, lying here on this couch

which was his bed; afraid of nameless things in the night. The witches and sheeted figures which had haunted his childhood changed later into unrecognizable shapes that moved slowly and mournfully in the darkness, swishing at the draperies, scraping a chair along the uneven floor, scratching at the windowpane. Now and then he would call out to this mother, his voice frightened and tentative in the dark, for reassurance. Many times he had sat upright, tense and breathless, listening, straining against the silence for a sound to give clue to the anonymous dread. Once he had heard his father calling in the night, once shortly after the suicide. But always in the morning the haunted room resumed its limpness: the lifeless chairs, the awkwardly-legged table with the crocheted doilies; morning sat ruthlessly and real on the plain furnishings and ghosts were untenable in the drabness.

Now the door was opening, the menace was actual and he did not move, did not even fear. His drained body watched with relaxation. The exterior threat come soundlessly through the door was relief after the hammering in the head; the film flickered and broke on the screen and the villain rose up comfortably in the next seat, human and controllable after all, cut down to normal size, comfort in the fingers that clutched at his throat. It would be the police, the taciturn, beefy men who ate pie to strengthen them against the criminal. He had left something behind; he had done something wrong. He thought with what seemed reasonable improbability that the picture of the girl on the desk had revealed his secret; that the innocent face had informed, speaking eagerly out of the joy of a First Communion day, truth white and round in the young mouth. He could deny the robbery now, he thought, and decided to stand up and say 'Here I am' and hold out his hands for the steel cuffs.

"Martin Lynn," a voice said. It did not sound official. In the moonlight he could see only a coat pocket and a hand hooked casually inside. The switch clicked and the lamp came up at the same time. "I remembered where it turned on," the man said, and seemed to smile as Martin blinked at him. He was tall and calm and wore a vivid suit; a discharge button gleamed dully in his lapel. "Martin Lynn, Junior," he said, turning toward the couch. He had a clipped, confident mustache, a physical ornateness which matched the loud clothing.

"What do you want?" Martin asked, sitting up in curiosity and not fear. He rubbed his eyes against the glare. "Are you a policeman?"

The man smiled, easily, winningly. "A policeman?" he echoed. "Whatever gave you an idea like that?" His voice was smooth and musical, arching flexibly into intonations; laughter slanted around the eyes. "You look—upset."

Martin was conscious of his hot, prickly body under the clothing he had forgotten to remove; his skin felt red and flushed; his trousers itched against his leg. My mother is dead, I have killed a man, he might explain, sifting the words casually toward the smiling stranger.

"It is, of course, an odd time to call," the man said. "But I saw you come in. I thought I might help you."

"Help me?" Martin asked. The numbness was passing now; he became wary. They had set somebody to follow him, after all. These policemen without uniforms might be everywhere, making up the ordinary scenery of a city street, the badge concealed, the hand ready to come down heavily on the shoulder from behind.

"I knew your father," the man said. "My name is Craig. I saw the cops with you in the diner. Once they begin to pursue, a man can't sleep; I know. You didn't do it, did you?"

"Do what?" Martin retreated behind questions, suspicious now of the smiling man who had known his father. His mother had always referred to his father's friends as "bad company." So many of them had been like this: handsome, smiling men in garish clothes with stickpins in their ties. He might still be a policeman; his father had known policemen, too.

The man shrugged. "Whatever they were asking about. It doesn't matter much what. Once they begin, they never stop." He glanced toward the inner room. "Is your mother here?"

Once in a rare moment of courage, his mother had impulsively told a group of his father's friends that she would pray for them. They had laughed, loudly, jesting in brass voices about it as they paddled down the steps afterwards. But they had not liked to see her after that. "She's dead," Martin said evenly. He remembered again the funeral, the inevitable sequel to the final gasp; remembered that Mrs. Lally had said the young priest had arranged for the funeral. Where had the young priest been during the murder? It would be cheap, he thought; the cheapest possible, the frail body banked eerily in the inexpensive coffin. "She died today."

"I'm sorry," the man named Craig said, softly, as though he honestly were. Martin was tempted suddenly to ask about his father, to try to pierce the mystery of the leap over the rail of the bridge, the shocking plunge into the fatal waters. His mother had only prayed and wept. He himself had been young, accepting the meagre explanations, watching his mother sorrowfully, moved more by her grief than by the occasion. "Is that what they wanted?" Craig said, after a silence. "The cops?"

"Them," said Martin. "They wanted to know about a robbery, a shooting. Something at the Galaxy Theatre. They tried to trick me into it."

"They'll trick everybody," Craig said. And then, lightly: "A shooting? Why did they ask you? Did they—did they see the criminal?"

"I don't know," Martin answered, "what they saw. They said I looked suspicious." He was aware of his hands again; they seemed huge, ungainly in his lap. He put one over the other, but it didn't help; they looked twice as big. He crossed his arms, nudged the hands under his armpits, feeling small and cold suddenly.

"It was a bad time to come," the man said, getting up. "I thought if I could help about the police— I liked your father. He used to talk about you a great deal."

"I didn't know him very well," Martin said, thinking he was close to his father now, in the same world with the glittering men who gambled, talked eagerly of horses and odds, ambled over sometimes into the world of the illegal. He was "bad company" himself now. "What—what did he say?"

"The usual things," Craig said. The conscious charm kept coming back into his voice. A wheedling, familiar tone that implied some hidden intimacy. "Said you were a fine boy; like your mother, he used to say. He was all right, Martin Lynn. Always a joke, always the bright side. He'd have given you the shirt off his back." Martin treasured the words; he had never heard his father's name before without regret and pity interlarding the words. "Martin Lynn's boy" people had said, shaking their heads. "He was a poor one." The old priest had looked at him the same way before he——

The stranger was at the door. "I'd better be going," he said. But hesitated. He had something in his hand, a square of paper. He started to put it back into his pocket, changed his mind again and withdrew it. He smiled.

"Here," he dropped the paper on the table. "Take this. It might come in handy." It was money, Martin saw, folded up into a wad. It uncurled when it fell to the table. A single bill.

Martin remained on the couch, staring at it. The markings were unfamiliar, the picture strange; a large denomination. He looked quizzically at Craig.

"It's nothing," Craig said. "If I can be of help, anytime—well, I'll be around." He moved gracefully out the door. A faint glow of perfume hung in the room behind him, sweet and pungent. His feet padded away down the stairs. Martin stared at the money for a long time before he moved to inspect it. Then he gasped. It was a fifty-dollar bill. He had never before seen so much money at one time. He began to calculate, standing breathlessly beside the table. He could rent a high-powered funeral car, put the money toward a more expensive casket. Grandeur danced in his head. He turned toward the inner room, pulled himself erect, and spoke to the curtains, as though his mother were beyond, standing frail and distracted beside her bed in yesterday's faded dress, as though death had intensified her indigence. "This is for you," he said, in twisted triumph. "It's all worked out all right."

2

The Thought

I

THE POLICE were in and out of the rectory half the night. "It'll be better if we do it now," the detective said. "In the daytime it would be a scandal." He was a tall, detached, preoccupied man, whose gaze went over your shoulder invariably. The young priest stood helplessly in the corridor as the mechanics of officialdom clattered around him. After the girl had gone, he had called the chancery and reported the incredible event; on a piece of paper from the desk pad he had scrawled, from telephone information, the name of the priest who would arrive tomorrow to take Father Kirkman's place, at least temporarily. It would mean two guest-priests for Sunday since one visitor was habitual.

The fact of death still rapped relentlessly on the door of his brain awaiting admittance. The hulk by the fireplace garnished with a blood rapidly becoming black in color suggested nothing of the gray old man who had taken lately to limping down the step; the old man who muttered solemnly over Mass every day, his girth bulking against the vestments; the old man who had sat opposite him at table for three years. The departure of the spirit drained the flesh of resemblance. The young priest whispered an incessant prayer as the coroner tramped through, followed by the photographers: the businesslike companions of death, reducing the fall by the hearth and the gasping and the silence to a matter of impersonal report.

"False teeth," the young priest heard somebody remark, coldly, without implication. Father Kirkman would no longer snore gently in the darkened hall upstairs as a late sick-call took the young priest softly out in the chill morning; would no longer expel his thick breath in the silence of the study as he scanned a sermon the young priest had planned for Sunday. Privation could only be imagined by contrast with plenitude; he could only visualize the old man's absence by recalling his presence, his gray, dim-eyed security which stood always as a support behind the young man's tentativeness. Mourning was like a pin caught in clothing, pricking at unexpected spots. Loss was not an emotion that repetition minimized.

"Whatever it was," the detective was saying, "it was heavy, and had a sharp edge on it." The young priest had read conditional prayers over a helpless form for the second time that evening. The soul might still have been imprisoned under the stained cassock, although the cerements of death hung white on the skin. It was the first time he had mouthed the prayers in their full meaning, applying the worn epithets to a decay he knew and loved. He shivered again, remembered how he had spoken lightly and jokingly of Father Kirkman at a recent meeting with a man he had known in the seminary. "The old fellow," he had called him. The surge of death engulfed the difference in their ages; they had been friends.

The detective, Mandel, came out in the corridor. Men were beginning to pack up their equipment, to straggle out and down the steps, talking sketchily. "There isn't much to go on," Mandel said, "but I guess we'll get him. In time."

It occurred to the young priest for the first time that a murderer was involved. Death had borrowed a body's disguise and come familiarly up the steps, perhaps smilingly into the room, shaking hands across the desk before the fatal blow. Someone had stood, heart beating deafeningly in his ears, and wielded Father Kirkman's doom. If the death itself was incredible, a dealer of death was preposterous.

"It's one o'clock now," Mandel said, looking at his watch. "It happened three to five hours ago, the doc says." He was an earnest, determined man, grimly searching the facts.

"We returned at twelve," the young priest said. He tried to remember a door slamming as he came in, a shape among the trees on the street, a car pulling away. Perhaps they had missed the criminal by minutes.

"It was a hard blow," Mandel said. "Behind the ear. Fairly heavy object. Fairly strong arm. I'd guess a man. But that's not definite." He faced the priest for a moment, then peered at the floor. "Would you rather talk about it tomorrow?"

"I hadn't thought," the priest said. "Now will do as well. I won't sleep."

They went into the room across the corridor from the study. It was sparsely furnished, with vacant stretches of polished wood. The chairs were the usual uncomfortable ones. Mandel sat fingering a notebook. The young priest looked out the uncurtained window.

"I never heard before of a priest being murdered," Mandel said.

"Murder," the young priest said, "is so personal, so— worldly. You need more life of your own than a priest has." He amended this in the face of fact. "Usually."

"I knew this man," Mandel said. "From the days I walked a beat. They used to assign me to the Holy Name Parade. The sergeant thought it promoted good will." He allowed a friendly silence to intervene. "Will you give me your full name, Father."

"Roth," the young priest said, watching the cars at the curb, a face peering out of an upper window across the street. "Aloysius Roth." He spelled both names. The questions seeped in among the broken chaos of his thoughts; he answered automatically. He tended to reject the possibility of a religious fanatic; Father Kirkman was such an infirm symbol of the Church. A thief? A housebreaker?

"Is it ridiculous to ask if he had any enemies?" Mandel intoned his litany of questions wearily, doggedly.

"It seems ridiculous to me," the young priest said. He couldn't imagine hate glinting out at the old man, anger alive against the peaceful face. But some dark emotion haunted the room. Out in the street he could see an ambulance with dim figures loading something in the back. He called to Mandel.

"We'll have to take him to the morgue tonight. Tomorrow wherever you say. Murray's, maybe?"

They closed the doors. The driver began to whistle as

he ground the motor into operation. The ambulance whirred away.

"What about the girl?" Mandel asked. "You said—his niece?"

"She's his only relative. There were some cousins in Germany, but they disappeared during the war."

"The girl," Mandel persisted. "Any bad blood there? It's most often families hate each other."

"There were differences," the young priest said. "He acted as her guardian sometimes, although she felt she didn't need one. I don't think it went to these extremes." How could one be sure of the extent of human malice now, he thought, when it was capable of killing Father Kirkman. How could you draw a line and say: this is possible, this is not. In the midst of life, we are in the midst of death. Around every corner.

"And of course you came back together," Mandel mused. "Unless she had an accomplice." The young priest was startled; his own theory of indiscriminate vigilance put suddenly into words. Mandel looked at the notebook and answered his glance. "We have to consider every possibility. This looks like an amateur's job. Where nothing's certain. We had another case tonight. At the Galaxy Theatre. That was done by a professional. An experienced criminal. It was worked out on a time schedule. This is different."

Father Roth thought what a comfort the "criminal" could be; not only to the police, but to everyone. A man moving in certain patterns, holding a defined place in the scheme of the world, given to certain violences by the clock, abiding by regular working hours. The considered, habitual sinner adept by practice and study. Nothing was upset by his depredations; statistics made them comfortable; the routine chugged on. He was explained by percentages. It was the instant, random sin that clogged the wheels; the respectable gone amuck; the elect deceived. The sudden smash of evil in the perfectly-appointed drawing room; the storm out of season, the time out of joint.

"Can you give me her address?" Mandel looked up wearily from the notebook, looked past him at a gaudily red St. Joseph impassive in the corner. "I'll have to question her."

"I don't know it," Father Roth said. Suppose she had had an accomplice; murder riding beside him in his car, sitting coolly in a corner of the leather seat, a shadow in the half-light. "She promised to call here tomorrow." She could, of course, be miles away by now with the big, gleaming man named Malcolm. He had, after all, no assurance.

"We'll be able to trace her if she doesn't turn up," Mandel said. He got to his feet, stuffed the notebook awkwardly into a pocket.

"If you think of anything else—any other little fact that might help. The most unlikely bits of information help; sometimes half the battle is recognizing a clue when you see one." He smiled humorlessly, as though to apologize for mouthing a precept of his profession. "Rita Conroy you said?"

"But I'm sure she'll come," the priest said. Why was he sure? Because he had vouched for her, had let her go down the stone steps and away when anything horrible was now utterly possible? Or because he believed ground-lessly in the eyes under the brisk hat, the determination in the lips which held a trait of Father Kirkman?

Then the phone rang. He excused himself and went into the corridor across to the study, toward it; hoping it was the girl.

"St. Stephen's," he told the mouthpiece. "Father Roth speaking."

"Father—Roth," a voice quivered across the wires. It was the girl. "This is Rita Conroy." She hadn't run, at any rate.

"Oh, yes," he said, rather cheerily, as though she were an old friend whose voice he hadn't heard for some time. "Yes."

"Has anything happened?" she asked. Mandel's mention of accomplice recurred to him. What might be in her mind behind the words?

"The police are here," he said. "They'd like to see you . . . to talk to you." His rephrasing seemed to soften the blow.

"Now?" she asked. "Should I come now?"

"I'm sure the morning will be all right." He called Mandel into the study and arranged a time. "They want your address," he told her. He scribbled it on the desk-pad as she gave it to him, ripped the page and passed it to Mandel.

She was saying something else, something that came with difficulty through the instrument. "I'm sorry . . ." She paused. "I apologize if I was rude this evening." Pride blurred the message; the effort of humility strained along the wires.

"Quite all right," he told her. "It seems unimportant now." He thought there would be nobody to interfere with her next attempt at marriage, nobody to offer the unwanted guidance to her sullen pride. "We must pray for him," he told her. There was a long silence. She said, "Goodnight" and the connection was blinked out. We must pray for you, too, he thought to himself.

Mandel struggled into a topcoat. He stood by the door, his impassive face shaded by his hat. "I'll come back in the morning," he said. "I'd like to talk to anybody who might help. Try to find out if anybody benefits by his death. A will."

"It's all impossible," Father Roth said, staring at the desk. "There can't be much money. Nobody stands to gain, materially or otherwise. Nobody had a reason; nobody could have had a reason."

"A looney then," Mandel said. He moved into the corridor, turned again at the door. "There's never any reason for these things. You can't count on that. It might just seem like a reason for two minutes." He had the door open now. "I'm leaving a man outside—just in case. We've been over the house. But you never know." He looked at the priest momentarily before his gaze drifted away toward the ceiling. "The murderer might still be around. He might come back. It might be—anybody." He mumbled a goodnight as the door closed behind him.

Father Roth went back into the study and stood staring at the empty chair. Nobody had anything to gain—unless it were himself; he might be pastor now. He prayed the thought away. It was unfeeling, callous, even to think it while the old body lay stripped of dignity in a morgue.

He could think of nothing he desired less—at such a price. Had the idea, he wondered as he clicked out the lights, occurred to Mandel?

II

Martin woke with the money clutched in his hand, woke stiff and sandy-eyed on the uncovered couch. The day squeezed as much light into the room as it ever could. For a moment, as he sat up, it was just a day, presenting the ordinary problems and the familiar terrors: his mother's patient weariness, the flower shop, the abrupt customers, the rush and honk of traffic, his fear of people, his self-consciousness. For a moment he adjusted himself to his customary dread. And then the vacuum of his memory was filled up as the pressure of the past bubbled in, swirlingly, gurgling up to the brim, seething inside him. The events moved forward in a mob and were vague horror and a nameless, unsettling fear before they assumed their own frightful and disgusting order. From cloudy disturbance he moved rapidly to a state of horrifying awareness; reality broke on him like a vision and he gasped, pressing the back of his wrist against his trembling mouth. He had killed; he had struck down in anger; he had spilt blood violently as the arm descended, as the teeth ground together.

His head pounded crazily. He rocked back and forth on the couch moaning as though he were in physical pain. He thought he was going to be sick again as the assault of reality exploded in his nerves and organs: the shock to the soul spending itself inside his bowels. But he was not. Nothing at all happened. He waited, still wailing brokenly, for the sharp edge of the pain to dull, for the realization—the huge, crushing, torturing fact—to blend gently into the furniture of his mind, to take the color of an acceptable thing and reside calmly; instead the weight seemed to increase. The face of his sin became more grotesque; instead of placidly taking its place in the crowd of its fellows in the comfortable distance, in the frame within which it is possible to perform the normal day, it increased in size, in evil, growing in him like an enormous balloon. It pressed against the sides of his brain. He could feel the gigantic horror pushing against the very skin of his head. Guilt like a tumor swelling inside him. Until he fell to the floor with a wild, high-pitched cry and lay gasping with his head tangled in the cloth of the table.

He thought eagerly that he might go insane, that the strain upon his mind could relieve itself only by extinction. The white dazzling shaft of light which sweated down on the floor of his consciousness to reveal the atrocities there, might be cut off abruptly, switched sharply away, leaving only a cool darkness and nothingness; a chill vacancy; the solace of oblivion where no toll was taken. He thought if he could crawl back into a corner of this cavernous room which was his mind, haunted by himself in various postures of disgrace, he would be invisible, blending into the shadows, making not even a lump in the gloom—that he might breathe easily again. He embraced the possibility and strained toward it; seeking a blackout where no shape would be distinguishable, no ghost awful and apparent. But the light streamed on;

the grotesque shapes swayed and bobbed in the huge room which had no doors. He ran back and forth flinging himself against the blank walls, recoiling momentarily and running again into the barrier, seeking insensibility, fighting simultaneously the tenacity of the flesh and the spirit. The light beat down; he could find no switch to extinguish it, no corner in which to hide from it. He and his sins with their great grinning faces were locked together in the empty room with the slick white walls and there was no escape.

He had been, he discovered, banging his head against the floor. When he sat up, disentangling his head from the table throw, all the objects in the room seemed outlined sharply with a fresh intensity. The couch, the chairs, the table, the meagre flowers on a window rack, the thin high radiator with its iron ribs, the bookcase with its few volumes—all had the sharpness of a perfectly-snapped photograph. He had disavowed nothing; reality returned with twice its strength, twice its energy for all his rejection. The world remained, the sin remained, he himself remained.

He remembered Craig then, as pleasant happenings struggle through the crust of memory to take their more permanent place beside the brutalities; remembered his smile, his ease, his grace. "Once they begin to pursue," Craig had said, "a man can't sleep—I know." And yet Craig had sat in the chair smiling, comfortably, the naked light streaming down on his soul, too, illuminating the obscene corners. Craig was able to walk gracefully, to leave a musk of laughter in the room after his departure. If he did really know what it was like, as he had said.

Martin drew himself up, supported himself on the table briefly as he recovered his breath and then marched stiffly into the small bathroom. He must not dwell on the past, he told his face in the mirror, must not linger in the unhealthy groves of memory where the poison grew. He must plan, must map out a future of security, of escape, of wariness. He remembered the two detectives, the girl in the dim photograph, Mrs. Lally—these were his enemies. Before these, he must present the casual, the untroubled façade. He laughed gutturally to himself as he thought of the girl; that was nonsense, of course. He must distinguish carefully between the misty shapes of his imagination—the denizens of the blank room—and the tangible world. The ghost of the haunted room could speak to no one but himself. The detectives were the real threats; they had seen him, said he looked "suspicious," taken his name and address, looked searchingly at him. How much had they seen? There was nothing to connect him with the old priest: the blood, the fingerprints, the name on the desk-pad—these were destroyed, out of mind, out of all sight, they were gone and could speak no more. He had to fear only himself. He laved his face in water, peering into the stained mirror; his grief would be excuse enough for the gaunt eyes, the haggardness in the pits of the cheeks. He had reason enough to look like one of his own ghostly imaginings.

He remembered the money. Mr. Swanson owed him twenty dollars for this week's pay—he tried to recall what day it was and decided uncertainly that it must be Saturday now. Swanson wouldn't dare dock him for absence because of his mother's death; decency exposed to public examination forced certain observances even in Swanson. In his pocket he had a couple of dollars. All together some seventy dollars. It would be some contribution toward the promise he had made his mother, the oath he had sworn in the dark death-room over the cold body. He could fulfill his determination.

An action was his need now. The muscles directed, the mind intent upon performances—this would cushion over the ragged points of his consciousness. He must be busy and shrewd; these were his cues now. He came into the outer room with a new firmness in his step, the shadow of the old fear which had pervaded his eyes displaced by a cunning, a sly confidence which he consciously practiced.

The thought formed slowly, out of the clouds of his mind, that he had warrant for a new independence, a discovery of self as history-making as any voyage into strange waters. As the crucifix was itself a symbol, he had used it as such, in a symbolic manner, to break the chains which had enslaved him. His fear of power, his cowered acceptance of precept, his cringe before whatever authority, were without basis now—now that the old priest had gone down leadenly behind the desk. The new Martin Lynn, he thought, applying the colored lettering of the advertisements to his life. He would no longer be frightened by myths perpetuated by mumbling old crones in darkened hallways. His mother's abjectness, his father's despair were historical events whose meaning could be read clearly. At the bottom of all the hocus-pocus, the ceremonies, the feudal tradition, stood at last the rock of the individual, the free self, capable of action, endowed with innumerable potentialities. Remorse carried with it a compensation of clarity; having gone all the way, accomplished the final, tempestuous deed, he had come through a curtain of darkness into the world of things as they were. His private ghosts had dispelled the misty apparitions that had discomforted his childhood; the incredible caricatures of sin, of hellfire, of mental inquisitions performed by accusing ecclesiastical shapes, dissolved before the concrete pursuer and the tangible future.

As he brushed his suit, he looked with new admiration at his own hands, for they seemed implements of adeptness, going surely about their business. They were his liberators, twin allies in the new dispensation. He drew himself stiffly up; it was seldom he had been meticulous about his appearance, preferring to blend always into backgrounds, to conceal the reticence of his fear in protective coloring, defensive carelessness. His suit, of course, was too small: narrower across the shoulders even than he was, short and tight at the shoe-tops, and out of prevailing fashion in the severe plainness of its cut. He combed his hair carefully, pushing with his hands against the untrained wisps which curled up and away from the crown of his scalp. He might at least afford what had been heretofore the luxury of a haircut in honor of the funeral.

He walked resolutely out the door, pulling it shut behind him with a slam and almost with a flourish. A strut marked his progress toward the stairs. What remained in him of grief at his mother's death was submerged now in the flood of importance his blow at tyranny had loosed.

The glamour bestowed by sorrow retired before the magnificence of the deed done and the challenge which still remained. He had freed himself; he would vindicate his mother's name. Not only murder; sacrilege as well. A luminous glory trailed after him in the stairwell.

And then Mrs. Lally's door swung softly open—did she crouch there interminably, awaiting the approaching footstep?—and the dark, bent figure urged forward through the half-light. His palms began to perspire.

"Martin," the cracked voice said, "Martin."

"Yes," he answered her roughly. She was the voice of poverty and insecurity, echoing the past.

"Are you all right?" she asked him. He could feel, rather than see the concern on the wrinkled face, the black arm straining toward him. "You came in so late. I worried." He could picture her lying always inside the flat, enlivening the night with stories spun out of the passing footsteps.

"I'm fine." He was brusque until he remembered that he must appear still the sorrowing son, the figure of pity and dependence. Any deviation from the passive norm might excite suspicion; might pass eventually through the mysterious channels of gossip to the ears of the police. He bowed his head. "I'm going to Murray's," he said. "I want to see her."

"Poor boy," the old lady said. There was a feeling of croon in the songless voice; it was more a suggestion than a reality, like an intention gone awry. "Poor boy." It was the same old thing, he thought, the pity that entrapped you if you listened to it long enough. "I'm coming over

this evening," she said patronizingly with the air of be-
stowing a favor he would be grateful for. "I'll stay with
you. Such a trying time."

He nodded rapidly and turned down the stairs. She
couldn't, of course, see him in the dark; or very well in
the light for that matter.

The changes in him—his confidence, his resolution—
were lost on her. The old do not recognize change when
it takes place; there is no tomorrow for them, only the
past repeating itself in various disguises; no adjustment
except the increase of the weight which is carried, the
burden which chisels the daily pattern deeper and shuts
out more light.

His spirits fell as he descended the steps. She had promised to come to the funeral home: he could see her beside
him at the casket, nodding and praying, the old head
wavering on the frail body, the black, cheap clothes making a mock of mourning. They would be twin figures of
poverty and discomfort. For the first time in his life he
swore, futilely and almost sobbingly—swore, and clenched
his hands and was desperate and alone and frightened
as he came out into the street.

He turned left along the pavement. Summer's grime
sprayed in visible, changing patterns before the erratic
October wind. He felt insignificant, unwashed, awkward.
As he passed the grocery store at the corner, two old men
in the shadow of its tattered awning exchanged gnarled
whispers. He reddened and walked faster. The poor Lynn
boy, he could hear them saying; imagined he could hear.
His hands were burdens again; the film began to dart and
flicker in his mind, re-enacting the murder. He slumped

furtively toward the funeral home, self-pity welling up in him like a saccharine liquid.

III

Malcolm had called twice during the night; once, shortly after Rita had come back to her apartment, when she had given him the facts and refused further conversation; again an hour or so later, the bell rioting through the quiet rooms and disturbing Mary Jane so that she tossed and sighed in the bedroom. The second time Rita had consented to meet him for breakfast. "Poor darling, you need me," he had said. And the resonant voice revived a world she had almost forgotten in the stress of the old man's dying: the world of ease and good living and soothing conversation that Father Roth had destroyed last night. It was still there, she thought, remembering Malcolm's voice, hers for acceptance now that the barriers were gone, the commandments voided, the old man dead. She did need him, she decided.

"Father Kirkman killed!" Mary Jane had looked at her with amazement, standing at the half-open door. They were queer roommates. Mary Jane was always the first to arise, the first to dress, the eager one, slipping with resignation into her simple, plain dresses and going off to Mass. She was stunned at the news; the inexplicable intruded rudely in the precise time-schedule of her simple devotion. "A good Catholic girl" Father Kirkman had called Mary Jane Glennon when he had proposed the arrangement as a thinly-disguised method of bringing virtuous influence to bear on Rita, and Mary Jane was. She

might have worn the words as a motto around her prim
hat. Her religion trotted at her heels like a pet dog, carefully groomed and fed, a well-mannered, characterless
animal with no nasty habits. "How awful," Mary Jane
had said of the murder. "It was only yesterday——" and
she launched into a mediocre reminiscence. Rita lay back
in bed resentfully watching Mary Jane smother the fact
with platitudes. "His was a beautiful soul," Mary Jane
said and went sorrowfully off to Mass, happy in her detached grief.

The comfort of the apartment and the respectability
of its address had made the arrangement feasible to Rita.
Mary Jane was easy to live with; a bore, of course, stocked
with innumerable illustrations of the cutenesses displayed
by the seventh-grade children she taught in the parish
school—a bore, but no trouble. They saw each other rarely
—when Rita returned early or rose early; their compati-
bility was based on mutual disappearance. It was Mary
Jane, Rita thought with a resignation that only the events
of the night before could have given her, who had told
Father Kirkman about the planned elopement; a com-
plexity of preparation had given her away. She wondered
suddenly, to her own surprise, whether Mary Jane's shield
of platitudes, the intricate design of folklore, weren't after
all the best defenses against both death and disappointment. Catholicism offered cheerfully to solve everything,
she reflected bitterly.

Sitting across from Malcolm at breakfast at a hotel
where they had agreed to meet, she decided Mary Jane
had no monopoly on refuges. "The unexpected not only
always happens but should be expected," he said, after

the barest of polite regrets. "I can't really go into mourning," he added with a petulant frankness. "After all, the old fellow was standing in the way of our happiness. The only personal emotion I had for him was dislike," the eyes suggested a smile which tempered the audacity, "tinged with repulsion."

"Please," she said, and found herself smiling and could not decide if her reluctance to share his levity was due to genuine dislike or merely another habit she had not quite outgrown.

"From his point of view it's desirable, isn't it? He'll go to heaven. Or at the very least purgatory."

"He's dead now," she murmured and remembered suddenly that murdering a priest was worse than murdering an ordinary man; his holy orders weighted down the offense, too.

"It would be hypocritical to pretend I'm sorry," Malcolm asserted righteously. "If it weren't for him, we'd be married right now—instead of eating breakfast."

"He's dead now," she repeated. "He's gone now. No barriers."

"None at all." She could be his wife now at any time; nothing stood in their way now. It was the first time her speculation on the possibility had been unimpeded; the first time she had clearly envisioned their marriage. The objections had loomed larger before, the difficulties had overwhelmed the deed, lending it enchantment, as a forbidden pool shimmers behind locked gates. Now the gates were wide and the water looked unbelievably normal. Pleasure, she had imagined; wit, security, comfort. And there was only the plain, clear fluid; no nectar at all.

"It would have been awkward if we had been married," Malcolm was saying. "To come back for the funeral and the investigations. I'm sure I shouldn't have been able to keep my mind on the service."

Would he have been killed, she asked herself, watching Malcolm smile, if they had not attempted marriage. She had wished the old priest dead often enough; wished him out of her life, away where she would be free. He might not, in the first place, have been left unprotected; that was a circumstantial probability. Was there another, some mystic, indefinable connection between her desires and the death; some dreadful juxtaposition of events which laid some of the sin on her? She shivered again; the old superstitions were hard to dispel.

"Catholics do bury, don't they?" Malcolm said.

"Of course."

"I thought they enclosed them in glass cases. I've read of saints like that." His face clouded as he looked at her; all his emotions were public, as though he himself were bound in a kind of cellophane. "I'm offending you."

"You're not at all," she said. But he was. The levity broke sullenly over her memories of her uncle, over this mysterious fear of some subtle connection with his death. She thought of him lying on the hearth with something like regret. Opposition had drawn them together. He had been her guardian since she was sixteen; that was ten years ago. Their war was long standing, for even when she came of age he had refused to relinquish his jurisdiction. For five years he had meddled at her life without excuse, shaking his gray head, reprimanding, warning, beseeching her in turns. A tie had been created; the evil that men do does live after them.

"I can't help being glad." Malcolm clasped her hand. "We're free of him now. Like the fairy stories. The ogre's dead."

"Please," she said again, this time crossly. "He was my uncle. The only relative I had." She wished she hadn't said that; it identified her with what she had for so long been trying to escape.

"You'll have me," Malcolm said. And she remembered how long and how often she had longed to hear him say these words; hoping he would hesitate in the middle of a jest to insert a word of love; how long she had waited before it came. He represented release and rescue for her, the answer, charming and dependable, to all the old priest's aphoristic mouthings. Now they fell curiously flat on her ears. She had him! But it seemed so little suddenly. When the vision was approached, the halo turned out to be only paint.

"We can be married any time," Malcolm was saying. "As soon as you feel it's—decent."

Outside the plate-glass window of the hotel dining room, a man shuffled along the pavement, an unshaven face partly visible above the upturned collar of a coat; he moved evilly, inhumanly. Somewhere her uncle's murderer, her wish's minion, moved likewise.

In addition to her uncle's objections, their wedding had been delayed also because Malcolm's divorce decree had not yet become final. "Today was the day for that," he said, jubilantly. "We were really taking a chance last night. The Providence of God."

Rita had met his first wife, a tall girl chipped from alabaster, pale and unbending and exquisite. "She could never find her bedroom slippers," Malcolm had commented, and remained characteristically vague about her. It had lasted two years. The girl already had plans for another marriage when they parted. "I couldn't really boast that she was wrapped up in me," Malcolm had admitted wryly, in another of his infrequent allusions.

"The police want to talk to me," she told him, purposely derailing her own train of disturbing thought. She tried to smile.

"Lord," Malcolm said. "I keep forgetting it's murder. Who do they suspect, the Communists or Jehovah's Witnesses?"

She was annoyed again, the spleen coming like a taste into her mouth. "Who else would murder a priest?" he said in mock incredulity. "Unless there's a Vatican NKVD that liquidates undesirable elements. Certainly from my point of view, your uncle was an undesirable element."

"You're not cheering me up if that's what you're trying to do," she said, and rose to her feet.

"Darling," he was beside her in a moment. "I'm sorry. It's only because I'm selfish about us. You know this talk is innocent. It's too early to be serious."

They exchanged the chastest of kisses as he put her into a cab. He stood hatless on the curb waving at her when the vehicle pulled away. Immediately he was out of sight, all her tenderness for him welled up. His joyous paganism had attracted her at once: he was the first man able to give clever and comforting reasons for her own chafings under the yoke of Catholicism. "It's all very well for old women who have no figures," he had told her, in a typical remonstrance, and ushered her into his own world of gaiety and badinage, touching her gently at the elbow as he guided her delicately away from the old beliefs into which she had been trapped.

In the cab, she was tempted to compare loves, ranging Malcolm beside the old priest who had threatened her with his daily prayers. She was afflicted with sadness at the realization that no one would be praying for her today, as the gray head bobbled over the altar stone and the lips uttered the interminable Latin, and in the cab she began to cry softly. Weeping at her own foolishness, the old man's foolishness, Malcolm's foolishness—she wasn't sure what.

When the cab arrived at the rectory, she was reminded that she had come to answer questions about a murder. It was incongruous to bracket the word with her uncle's name, his abstract world plunged suddenly into violence. She tried to remember if her own rage at him had ever boiled itself to proportions capable of this act of destruction. The murderer was unknown and the police would be seeking motives, enemies; certainly she qualified: they had been enemies all right, her own impetuosity at war with the old man's patience and rabid concern. How odd if they should suspect her. The sin of the heart proclaimed baldly in the courtroom. "Did you ever wish him dead?" "Yes, I wished him dead." And the word "Guilty!" reverberating through the room, spoken resoundingly by the judge behind the high paneled desk.

But, of course, she had an alibi. The jargon of movie gangsterdom came glibly to her mind. The young priest himself had been with her part of the evening. The irony presented itself to her as she absently paid the driver and turned to ascend the curved steps: the minister of God could avouch her innocence of the act itself. She had been committing another sin, another place, putting asunder what some other nearsighted justice of the peace had put together with faulty stitches.

But another factor presented itself. The young priest had said he would not reveal the events of the previous evening—if it could possibly be helped. Her alibi would be perfect only if the old man's disgrace were made public. "The murdered clergyman's niece was, at the very moment of his death, being married in a civil ceremony. . . ." She wondered if the Church, with its strange set of antiquated values, ranked scandal as a grosser sin than murder. She hoped she would see the young priest—what had his name been?—before she was questioned by the police. She was involved in a kind of Catholic conspiracy, her uncle's influence extending over the gulf of the grave to prolong an allegiance she had attempted so often to shake away from. She rang the bell and waited, watching the shadow of the church building next door as it fell across the sidewalk, the fuzzy outline of its slanted roof culminating in a cross.

IV

"Flowers," Martin told the florist, standing defiantly in the middle of the shop, among the suspended pots, overflowing with green, the clusters of colors in vases, the mixed odor of various sweetnesses. "I want a lot of flowers.

I don't care how much it costs. I'll work it off. No matter how many weeks."

"You misjudge me, my lad," Mr. Swanson said. He tried to keep his voice melodious; he felt it encouraged patronage. "I intended to send flowers. You're a member of the organization."

"I don't want just anything," Martin said. Not the usual stuff. I've seen the wreaths you make up. I want to fill up the room at Murray's. You let me pick 'em out and you can take it out of my salary."

"Your mother was a good woman," Mr. Swanson said. "The mother is the most respected of people. But we must keep our heads even in our grief." He smiled fondly at Martin, placed a fatherly hand on the boy's shoulder. "You don't have to prove you love her by burdening yourself with a bill like that. She would understand."

Martin shook off the hand. "Won't you let me do it? Won't you let me work off the money?" It was the first time he had ever said anything more than "Yes, sir" to Mr. Swanson. The effort of will tinged his face with strain, lifted his voice into a high register.

"It is good business for me," Mr. Swanson said. "Bad business for you. Let me send the flowers. Come back when you are yourself. Your job is here for you."

"Look," Martin said stubbornly. The anger was wadding up in his throat again, stringing his voice higher still, to the pitch of hysteria. "I'm not a child. I do things." Swanson stood looking at him paternally, understandingly, the superiority leaking out of his homely face. Swanson knew about his draft classification, his father's leap into the dark, his mother's poverty; pity wept at Martin out

85

of the older man's eyes. "It's not that I haven't got money, either," Martin thrust out the fifty dollar bill, his hand trembling. "But I need this for Murray's. I don't want any favors. Just a business arrangement."

Swanson was disturbed all right. The money made him take notice. Martin stepped close to him pressing his advantage. "Is it okay? Will you do it?" He was conscious of the hair scraggling around his ears; he felt unkempt among the neat floral displays.

"You're overwrought," said Mr. Swanson. "But if it's what you want, I'll do it, of course."

"Fifty dollars' worth," Martin's voice subsided into aspirateness. "In two months, I'll make it up."

"Take it easy," Swanson said. "You're speaking loud. There are customers. I'll do it. I'll do it."

Two women had come into the shop. They waited impatiently among the chrysanthemums. They were well dressed, jeweled, carrying an air of affluence; typical of Swanson's customers. Martin was aware of his shabbiness; appearances betrayed him like a loud, unsubtle friend, clapping him on the back and announcing his secret to the world raucously. He put away the money and began to edge toward the rear of the shop, toward the door he ordinarily used to load the delivery truck in the discharge of his duties. But suddenly he thought of the exit as another betrayal; another advertisement of his inferiority. He barged toward the front of the shop, brushing past Mr. Swanson and the women, rudely, scattering petals from a stem that arched into his path. At the door he turned, shouted to Mr. Swanson. "I want them there today," he said, "at Murray's."

He was glad when Mr. Swanson winced in embarrassment before the customers and he carried the image of it with him like a trophy as he walked rapidly along the street. This was not like the incident with Mrs. Lally; he had got through this one with honor. He had risen above the shame of his heritage, vindicated in some indefinable manner the honor of his family. Pride burned in him like a fire. He was proving himself; he had made a promise and it was indelible.

He thought of Craig and was grateful toward the smiling man with the crinkle of humor hard-bitten around the eyes. Without the money, his resolutions might have waned; with it, he was able to meet all opponents on an equal footing. Money was the secret; any fool could see that. He would make sure he had it from now on. There were ways of getting it; Craig could probably help. And after last night—the sequence of events began to unwind itself again, throbbing in his head as he moved along. Well, he had been brave then, too; he had stood up to the old priest. In a way, it was the beginning of everything, it was the initial strength. The Church was the fiercest opponent, snatching at your mind, forcing obedience by threats, preaching poverty to make you submit, squeezing the spirit dry and limp on the rack of penance and fear. He had struck out at the Church and driven it down in a dark heap on the hearth and the violence had lessened his subjection. With every move now, he gained more and more of himself, spread the wings of himself wider, occupied a larger area of the place which was properly his. He could ignore the old men who commiserated over him in doorways, the heads that wobbled in pity. They could pity themselves now, all of them, now that he was finding himself.

The figures in the film were confused then of a sudden, with the abruptness of transition his thoughts had been prone to ever since last night. He was standing behind the priest as before, lifting his hand with the crucifix higher and higher, all as before, when somebody stood between them. His mother stepped into the scene and raised flat hands against him, impeding him, stopping him, crying out in a way that froze his blood. He stopped in the street and shook his head, as though he could dispel the images; put his hands to his forehead and tried to wiggle his head to blankness. A girl passed him, staring curiously and his self-consciousness overbore the horror of the imagination. He looked up. He was standing in front of the Galaxy Theatre. The bare, unlighted lobby, cold and lonesome with chrome, was deserted; it was like an empty cave opening off from the sidewalk. The box office, a glassed octagon with barred windows, rose like a stalagmite from the center of the stone floor. Bits of paper blew up and down in the morning wind, plastered now and again against the photographs that were displayed in flat cases along each side; like primitive scrawls on prehistoric dwellings. He wandered inside, thinking that sin had made at least one more stop last night besides its visit to the rectory. The devil had stirred here, too, standing behind somebody just outside the grill and whispering hate into another ear. He stood over against the wall halfway between the doors to the interior and the mouth of the cavern, looking at the ticket-window. Had the detectives said what the weapon was here? A gun shot, they'd said. It was more efficient, impersonal, obviating the close contact, the acquiescence of the smote flesh and the collapsed bone. A gun sprayed death from a comfortable distance, magically and mechanically, and was too quick for groans.

He thought, suppose the old priest had lain moaning and bleeding on the hearth, the life only half out and pain scarring the old face? What would he have done then? Could he have moved in even closer with the crucifix, battering at the reluctant soul again and again? Martin shuddered in the cold, high place of echoes and wished that nothing had ever happened; wished he were caught still in the monotonous round of his deliveries for Swanson, flowers for other people's griefs.

Footsteps echoed in from the street. He could see the outline of a figure growing larger and larger between him and the light outside. He turned quickly and pretended to be looking at the colored photographs; arrested, flattering moments out of the darting story of the feature film. "The Avenger," the title smeared across the billboard in big black lettering. "Daring Drama of Intrigue and Passion" another line read. The footsteps sounded louder and louder through the cave, multiplying as the sounds bounded back from the closed end and returned to meet the new ones. "Flaming Love" the captions said; "Breath-taking Thrills." A squat menacing man in a black suit, his hand thrust ominously into his coat pocket, threatened a girl. The girl in a red dress stood on tiptoe on what seemed to be a hilltop; her arms were outflung and down, her head thrown back and the mass of hair streaming. Like a radiator cap, Martin thought. But she was beautiful. She looked like flaming love, all right. The footfalls were all around him in the air now, resounding from one wall to the other, mingling in a hollow tap dance inside his head. The figure was opposite him, somewhere behind him. The police? He turned and started slowly down the slight slope of the stone lobby, attempting to move casually, loafingly. The footsteps had stopped now, and he was nearing the opening, his own feet advancing closer and closer to the tide of sunlight which fell at an angle under the marquee and up toward him. His shoes moved into the brightness —and a voice called, from behind him and up.

"Just a moment," the voice said. It seemed important to him to pretend he hadn't heard the call. To keep on going. But the footsteps began again and the voice repeated and he stood where he was, halfway out into the sunshine. The echoes were less distinct out here, the reverberations fading off into the free air.

"Look here, young man," the voice said. It was beside him now. It was a calm, preoccupied voice, like that of a man who has looked up from a book. Its owner's interest seemed to be centered some other place than in the words themselves. "Have you seen——"

The voice trailed away, not cutting off abruptly. The man was behind him and Martin turned to face him. "Oh," the man said, as though he had made a mistake. He was tall, thin, quietly dressed; his hands hung limply by his sides; there was nothing of menace in him.

"Did you call me?" Martin asked and his attempt to be brash trembled and the cavern magnified his unsteadiness.

"I thought you were someone else," the man said, vaguely.

Long thin fingers adjusted his tie; in the dimness it was difficult to see his face. "Do you—," the man seemed to hesitate in embarrassment, "—live around here?"

"Not far," Martin said, thinking: more questions. The questions are beginning again; questions from strangers. He peered up into the gloom searching for some clue to his questioner's identity, to his profession.

"Something happened here last night," the thin man said. "Right here in this lobby."

"I heard about it," Martin said. "But I'm sorry——"

"Did you read it in the papers," the man wanted to know. His hands hung at his sides again as though they were uncomfortable doing nothing; he stared at something over Martin's shoulder, out into the street.

"Somebody told me," Martin said. "I've got to go now."

He took a step toward the street. But the man came with him. "And you still came in to look at the pictures?" the man asked. "After the—" he paused before the next word, held it deliberately in his mouth for a moment, "—shooting?" The word came out brittle. Martin had the sensation of seeing it fall to the stone paving with a clink as though it were lead. It lay there staring up at him saying murder, murder, murder. He felt the crucifix chill in his hand, saw the gray head shaking sadly as though in pity.

"Who are you?" Martin said. "What are you asking me that for?"

"I didn't ask much," the man said in a hurt, surprised tone.

"I don't know anything about any . . . murder," Martin

said, his voice wavering over the word, as though choosing it unwillingly because it was the only word that would do even though it was hateful to him.

"I didn't say murder," the man said mildly. Martin felt himself pale.

"Breath-taking thrills . . . passion and intrigue," Martin read from the billboard behind the man. "I'm a detective. I'm supposed to find out." This could be the end of his own private film, Martin thought—the last reel. He could say, casually, quietly, *I'm a murderer. I'm surprised you didn't recognize me,* and put out his hands for the manacles. The police were like God; everywhere, in the most ridiculous disguises.

"It's not easy," the man said. They were like old friends, trapped by intimacy. Martin measured the distance to the open street. Five steps, or six maybe. People hurried along to work in the sunlight. If he moved again, would the footsteps come with him, clomping along the sidewalk in the sun? "Last night there were two big jobs in this precinct; not five blocks apart. And nothing to go on. A man's supposed to be a magician." He scratched the back of his neck, then seemed to catch himself, to withdraw the hand shyly. "Oh, I'm not complaining. We'll find the criminals. But it takes so long; so much worry. No sleep at night. What's your name?"

Martin considered saying: "They've got my name. They got it last night over a piece of pie." But he didn't. He thought: the same detective working on both cases, the same man tying up the loose ends. The thought was frightening somehow so that he mumbled his name inaudibly and had to repeat it.

"Martin Lynn," the detective said. "You never know who's going to be of help, Martin." He smiled slightly, barely a smile; it was carefully restricted to his lips; his eyes continued to squint vaguely into distance. "You'd better tell me where you live."

Martin told him and the detective repeated it after him, airily, with a sort of awe, as though it were the first address he'd ever heard. "Fourth Street," he said again. "Who knows, Martin, maybe you can help me some day. All this crime. It gets—complicated." He smiled the narrow, humorless smile.

Martin nodded his head, trying to smile back. "I've got to go," he said, feeling cold and alone in the cave of the lobby. "I've got to go." He moved out into the sunlight. The voice followed him but the footsteps did not. The voice said: "You never know who'll help," followed, as he joined the stream of pedestrians, moving doggedly toward employment. I'm a murderer, Martin thought, and I walk along just as they do. There's nothing different about me; nobody can tell. It feels to me as though it should show somewhere, but it doesn't.

At an intersection he stood on the curb waiting for the light to turn green. I obey the lights, he thought; the minor laws are sacred to me. I have defied God and the police but I don't dare cross against the light. The cars swished and roared along the asphalt, their metal rattling at the speed. Their weight and momentum impressed him and he watched one after another in fascination. They had a doom in them too. If he took a step now, the brakes would grind and the tires would squeal and he would smash against the bumpers, making a squishy sound like the

crucifix had made on Father Kirkman; his body dragged
and mangled under the wheels. It was one way if they
got too close; if too many detectives came up to him and
asked his name, prying and probing. But first he had to
arrange about the funeral, bring his mother the fulfillment
of the vow made in the darkness, the promise of vindica-
tion. Then, possibly, the swift lunge off the curb, the defiance thrown into the round red eye that regulated these
monstrous machines. Like father, like son; guilt would do
for them both.

The lights changed and he moved mechanically with
the crowd. Again muscular activity switched and cheered
his thoughts. After all, though, he had behaved himself
very well with this last detective. He had revealed nothing,
suggested nothing, betrayed nothing. Nobody had to pity
him any more. He could take care of himself.

V

"Mandel's late," the young priest said. It was after nine
o'clock. He and the girl stood awkwardly in the small
front room opposite the study. All morning the phone had
been ringing, the doorbell buzzing, as parishioners veri-
fied the shock in awed, mechanical voices. A substitute
priest had said the second Mass, pronounced strained
condolence over a stunned breakfast table and gone away.
The young priest had never felt so young; the peace of
Mass had been partially dispelled at the morning meal
where Father Kirkman's chair sat lonesomely facing the
table. The housekeeper had laid the accustomed place

before the young priest had come downstairs to tell her it would not be necessary.

The old priest was deader in the daytime; where familiar associations hung about the corridors, padded heavily up the stairs.

Death was like an intermission at first, the emotions suspended with the event; the reactions slowed and hindered so that the pain, the loss was bearable. Feeling drifted back into the system slowly like a cloud of smoke, returned gradually and meticulously exactly in proportions the mind could withstand without complete befuddlement. One remembered the dead, not abstractly, but in concrete attitudes; memory retained the sense impressions which were the very doors of knowledge. Father Kirkman mouthing the prayers at the foot of the altar in an unintelligible monotone, giving full voice only to words at the beginning of phrases when he took a breath; Father Kirkman surrounded by children in the schoolyard at noon, his cape fluttering about his shoulders, a huge owl among sparrows; Father Kirkman emerging wearily from the confessional late on a Saturday night. The memories were anti-climaxes always. With an effort he could recall the high- and turning-points, but the minor moments presented themselves readily, added up by accumulations to the man he admired and loved. As long as the old priest was alive, the incidents had no value since they were repeatable, readily available in every day's routine. Now he was dead, the odd moments were rare editions, no longer obtainable.

Anger urged itself on him, born stubbornly out of his own sense of loss—anger and a temptation to revenge. The murderer must be found. Automatically he pictured a lean, cretinous face above stained clothing: a conception of "murderer" pieced randomly from newspaper photographs. His blame went instinctively toward the type. But Mandel had said: "It might be anybody." He remembered the words dully, tonelessly, as the detective had spoken them. Anybody! Mrs. Greer, the housekeeper; Pat Scully, the sexton; the girl! He looked angrily toward her, the accusation springing unbidden to his lips, the muscles tensing. She stood calmly by the window, impeccably dressed, maddeningly neat and trim in the bare room; she had the vacuity and deliberate unconcern of a fashion advertisement.

"Miss Conroy," he found himself shouting at her, a kind of savagery overlying the words. The outburst recalled him to himself, to his duties, his discipline, and he could not go on. The doorbell rang almost at once, filling in the silence his cry had emphasized. "Perhaps it's Mandel now," he said in a low empty voice and was ashamed of his anger. He tried to imagine Father Kirkman in similar circumstances: calm, patient, kindly, the old eyes blinking peacefully behind the glasses. Nevertheless, the anger served a purpose; he came to a decision. "I'm going to tell him about last night," he said, and was surprised that he spoke kindly. "We must do all we can to help."

Mandel came in vaguely, not looking directly at the girl. He acknowledged the introduction with a nod that was curt in its effect. "That's your picture on your uncle's desk, isn't it?" he said. "The same eyes."

The girl was puzzled. "Your First Communion picture," the young priest said. "Father Kirkman prized it."

She nodded slowly. Mandel ran through the usual series of questions, which the girl answered rather primly. Her mind appeared to be elsewhere, although she spoke without hesitation—until Mandel inquired about last night.

"Perhaps," the young priest said, "I can help here. We'd appreciate it if this didn't get out—to the papers or anywhere." He looked meaningfully at the girl. "Out of respect to Father Kirkman." Mandel nodded, continued to look indifferent, detached. "Miss Conroy," the young priest began, "had made plans to be married last night—in a civil ceremony. Since this is contrary to the laws of the Church, her uncle was distressed." She had not dropped her eyes; she was staring straight at him, in cold composure, as though curious about how he would say it. "When I came back from administering the Last Sacraments to a parishioner, he asked me to go after her and try to dissuade her. I left here about eight-thirty—they were to be married across the state line. Belleville. I got there about ten—and—" he glanced briefly at the girl, "I was in time. We returned here at midnight." Mandel made no notes. He stared abstractedly at St. Joseph in the corner.

"You must have broken the speed laws on your way out," Mandel murmured.

"Possibly." The girl had lowered her eyes now, slowly, without hurry, to inspect her wrist watch.

"Are you still going to be married, Miss—" Mandel consulted his book. "—Miss Conroy? After a while, I mean?"

In the silence, the young priest could hear his own breathing heaving jerkily in his chest. The girl did not stir. Mandel was staring steadily at the end of his pencil, turning it in his hand and squinting at it. It was a test somehow, the question—a test of the old priest's power, of the girl's loyalty, of the state of her soul on this bright morning when the sun poured into the window and glistened on the polished floor and on an old man's blood-stained shadow on the hearth.

"Yes," the girl said softly, "I'm going to be married."

The priest prayed, seeking grace for the young independence seated on the hard rectory chair.

"Are you glad he's dead?" Mandel asked, and the words came out calmly and coolly into the quiet room and did not explode until their echo took full force in the ear; as though a bomb shaped like a toy rolled awkwardly in at the door and unexpectedly tore itself apart.

"Damn you!" the girl said, standing up, the meticulous posture dissolving as passion molded the attitude ungracefully. "You have no right to say that."

"I'm trying to find a murderer," Mandel said, almost plaintively. "The murderer of your uncle. It's a simple enough question. You were miles away at the time. You have a priest's word for it. All I want to know is——"

"Then I'm glad." The girl's voice came low and intense, propelled by anger. "I'm glad. Who wouldn't be? All my life he's hounded me, blocking me at every step. Getting in my way. Interrupting my life. Who wouldn't be?" And then she wept, falling loosely back into the chair, collapsing completely whatever remained of the illusion of the distant and impervious young woman; she wept like the large-eyed child in the photograph.

"Please," the young priest said.

"That's all I wanted to know," Mandel said, getting to his feet, slapping the notebook shut. He looked shyly at the young priest. "I've got something, Father. We questioned the neighbors. A woman across the street said she saw somebody come in here about nine o'clock last night. A man, she said. She's nearsighted of course." His dry tone was resigned to impediments. "About five eight, thin, no hat, not well-dressed—as well as we can figure. She didn't see him go out. Another man rang the bell about twenty minutes later and got no answer. It sets the time better anyway."

He ambled toward the door. "The housekeeper who let me in—I'd like to talk to her." Father Roth followed him into the corridor, closing the door behind them, pulling it softly to on the child sobbing lonesomely on the chair. As they went toward the kitchen, Mandel spoke again. "Sorry, Father. I had to get some idea of what she was like." The priest nodded. Mandel threw his head back as the two of them moved along the hall, through the swinging door, "I often wonder," he said, "How these things come to you in the confessional. What the sin is like described in retrospect." The priest introduced him to Mrs. Greer and came away.

There was a formula, he answered Mandel's speculation for himself; there was a code: all the passion and the pride squeezed drily into categories; like profanity in a foreign language. The formal phrases stressed the effect rather than the deed; they had to do with remorse rather than description. The translation of the confession had to do with the echo in eternity.

The girl was standing in the corridor when he returned, standing composed and lacquered with no trace of tears

99

on her glass face. She said: "That was hardly fair, was it? I have reason enough certainly."

The young priest sighed. "Reason," he repeated vaguely. His own affection for the dead man rose in defense. "You can't believe he loved you. Love isn't indulgence, acquiescence. You can get acquiescence anywhere. From your enemies."

"In a way I'm sorry," she said, tracing her own line of thought, as though with a reminiscent finger, picking out a bright thread in a drab weave. "Naturally I'm sorry he's dead. But it would be untrue to say I'm not glad in another way—maybe a more important way. If it had to be like this, to let me make my own decisions." She looked at him frankly. "I do have to make my own decisions, don't I? You believe that. Free will."

"Yes," he said. "Goodness cannot be commanded." He thought how strong virtue was immediately after betrayal —Judas saying, "Why should not this ointment have been sold and the money given to the poor?" Aware of defection in one quarter—at least one—the girl clung to the righteousness in another. "I believe that," he told her. "But not that by itself; not only that." He wished for a new gift of tongues to condense the whole body of belief into a word that would catch at her as she turned to the door, that would spin her around and confront her with God and crack the composure; a magic sesame to mother the orphan of truth which stood so proudly in her, the lonely virtue gathering its strength in isolation. But nothing came. One had to go so far back to find agreement. But she paused, anyway; paused and turned and revealed embarrassment timidly breaking through the marble poise.

"The picture," she said. "Could I see it?"

He led her wordlessly into the study where daylight and the sun through the drawn blinds attempted to restore normalcy. In a moment of oblivion, he was surprised to find Father Kirkman's chair empty, but he remembered death quickly enough. He crossed to the desk and plucked the photograph from the blotter. Father Kirkman had shown this to him last night, in partial explanation, had held it in his hand as he talked, looking at it fondly, as though trying to reconcile the pictured innocence with the woman he could no longer comprehend. He had cracked the board in his agitation and the puffed, broken line showed now beside the young face, ruffling the white dress, the vague background.

Rita took the picture gingerly as though it were an insect, not looking at it until she held it in her hands. Then she kept it at waist-height, bending her keen, proud features down to it as if to conceal the recollection it implored.

"You might have been a bride," the priest said, risking the weak appeal, offered a hand across the gap of years, the hollows of sin.

Rita turned her large eyes to him distantly, with reassurance; she had met the ghost and she had not been afraid. The large-eyed girl in the fuzzy, brownish picture was a stranger she inspected critically and passed over, in the same way she might have looked at another beautiful woman for signs of superiority and been comforted by her own advantage. She smiled patronizingly. "Such a strange young girl," she said. The smile remained on her face as she turned to go.

He called after her. "You'll come to the funeral home?"

he said. "He'll be there instead of in the church. Forty Hours' Adoration begins Sunday."

"I'll try." It was a duty she must perform. "Is there anything else I should do?"

"There's nothing," he told her. "Nothing . . . except prayer."

He remained in the study as the door closed, as the glass rattled lightly, as the sound of her heels receded down the steps and was muffled in the street noises. He wondered how soon the wedding plans would go forward, whether the civil formality mattered, after all, a great deal to the proud, immaculate young woman and the inordinately confident young man. Perhaps his wild ride into the next state had been in vain; perhaps if he had stayed behind, he would have been in this room when the murderer arrived, could have intercepted the violence at the desk.

Mandel came back. "Not much there," he said, and relaxed onto a chair. "I didn't sleep much. We checked the lawyers early this morning. It doesn't amount to much, either. Father Kirkman administered the girl's money until she came of age. He had some himself once; must have been a fairly wealthy family."

The priest admired the efficient mind which examined the dust and debris of a lifetime in the search for sense, for order. "He leaves you some money," Mandel looked off out the window. "For those in distress, the clause reads. And the housekeeper and the sexton and a few odd persons here and there; there's insurance for the funeral and a provision it be kept small. Nowhere enough money for murder."

The details tried to narrow down the grief, to reduce

it to routine. Father Kirkman's was one among many, part of a crowd of souls storming heaven, each with its separate judgment, each with its separate alibi. But it retained uniqueness, nonetheless, the priest thought; the sparrow, the hair of the head.

"Do you know a boy named Martin Lynn?" Mandel asked. "He lives around here; he's in the parish. Maybe not a boy; nineteen or twenty."

"Lynn," the young priest remembered the frowzy apartment, the dark stairs, the old body on the bed. "Of course. His mother died recently—last night." It seemed long ago now, the events squeezed tightly into the hours. "That's where I was before Father Kirkman sent me—after the girl. A neighbor had called me, but I didn't see the son. He wasn't home."

"His mother dead," Mandel reflected. "So that's it."

"Is there a connection?"

"I met him on my way here. At the Galaxy Theatre where the robbery was last night." Mandel recalled the tortured young face, the fear signalling in the eyes—the fear which might have been grief. "For a minute late last night, I had an idea the two crimes might be related." He smiled up at the priest, blinked. "Guess I was just trying to simplify my job." He went toward the door. "I knew Martin Lynn's father. He had a record—a mild record—before he jumped into the river." He stopped with his hand on the knob. "I guess you'd say there's a connection between everything; every crime hooked onto another one somehow."

Sin hooked onto sin, the priest thought, like an endless train; wound one unto the other, all of them touching somewhere. The brass crucifix gleamed dully in the shaded sunlight, the thorns pricking up delicately from the bowed head. The thorns of sin interwoven, entangled, sharp, he thought—all related, like successive generations of a family exhibiting stubbornly a disfiguring trait. He said "Yes" simply and reminded himself to visit Martin Lynn, to offer consolation; and to remember the old lady in tomorrow's Mass.

VI

"J. T. Murray & Son, Thoughtful Service" the green neon lights arched out over the sidewalk; they were faded and soiled-looking in daylight. Beside the door, a plaque set into the wall repeated the message with more formality. A sign for the vulgar and one for the refined, Martin thought, as he pressed the bell. The autumn wind was canceling out the warmth of the sun and he found himself shivering in his tightly-fitted suit. He jammed his hands into his pockets and set his feet apart, jutting his chin up toward the glass-panelled, severely-curtained door. The house had all the incongruous dignity of a gravestone, set pat into the earth; the familiar paraphernalia of doors, windows, porch were altered ominously by the deathly dedication. Even the tube lights and the metal lettering and the folded awning did not disguise its concern with the dead. It was more than the empty eyes of the blinded windows, too; it had a character. Like me, he thought, it is identified with death.

He clutched the fifty-dollar bill in his pocket. He would spend it here, offering it for a more decorative casket, a finer lining, more brilliant brass handles, a higher array of candles; he would buy for his mother's final appearance some sprig of glory.

The door was opened by a young, fleshy man in black overalls, who said: "Yes?" while other, less polite inquiries darted from his watery eyes.

Martin found his throat dry, the words guttering out: "My mother's here," he said, "Mrs. Martin Lynn." The words themselves were pale and cold, dying out weakly against the young man's efficiency. "I came about arrangements."

The man in black maintained his attitude of listening even after Martin had finished speaking, as though surely he were going to hear something more important than this, then he assumed an air of practiced benevolence. "I'm sure you've nothing to worry about," he said. "This is a rather bad time and in any case, Father Roth made all the arrangements last night."

The name stirred among Martin's memories. The old priest had said: "Father Roth can preach you a sermon. . . ." Then he was the one who had come last night at Mrs. Lally's bidding, come while Martin roamed the streets in grief and indecision. They had exchanged locations, one to solace death, the other to seek it.

"I don't want a pauper's funeral," Martin said loudly. "I'll make my own arrangements."

The man in black was pained. He looked nervously behind Martin as though the reputation of J. T. Murray's had been threatened. He's the "& Son" Martin thought; the successful young executive. "Please step in," the voice flowed liquidly out through the automatic smile which was surreptitiously employed now. "Please step in and we'll talk it over." He pulled the door wide and stepped behind it, moving nimbly, loosely on rubber soles. Martin entered shyly and suspiciously, summoning his brashness, reminding himself of freedom.

Down a long, narrow hall beside a staircase, the man in black led him, his shoes whisking against the carpet, through a cool, high dimness and a musk of flowers. Chemicals lingered in the air of the small bright office to which they came, an acrid odor filming over the desks, the file cabinets, a big blowzy girl with panels of black hair dangling beside her face.

"This is Mr.—" the young man's voice began warmly, but altered to a pitch of doubtful annoyance at the name, "—Lynn."

"Who do I talk to?" Martin said belligerently, facing both of them. "I want to get some things straight. Where's J. T. Murray?"

"What's eating him, Albert?" the girl said.

"Either of us can take care of you," Albert said petulantly. He looked at the girl. "He was shouting at the front door. Making a scene."

"I'll shout a lot," Martin said. "Scenes. I can make scenes."

"This," Albert said, with abrupt reverence, "is hardly the place for them."

He folded his hands at his waist and pursed his lips and stood stiffly, like a schoolteacher or a maiden aunt, showering disapproval from his eyes. "I'm sure everything can be arranged in an orderly fashion. Now what seems to be the trouble?"

The blowzy girl was chewing gum deliberately, with

concentration. "Mrs. Lynn's downstairs," she said, without taking her eyes off Martin. "The kid's upset, I guess."

The young man became more flexible, leaned forward benevolently, smiled with an attempt at understanding; he had changed character again. The phrases were sprayed with syrup. "No one appreciates as we do the difficulties of the bereaved," he said. "The shock to the emotional system naturally results in short temper, undue displays of feeling, untoward incidents. But you must realize this is our responsibility now. You leave it in our hands. I assure you, many, many people have done so with perfect confidence." He continued to beam.

"I want to talk business," Martin said. "Save the sales talk." He moved to the desk, looked roughly down at the girl. "I don't know what that priest said, but I want a big funeral. I want the best of everything. All the trimmings. I'm prepared to pay."

He detected sympathy in the girl's eyes. They were ringed with mascara; rouge was spread in thick ovals on her cheeks; the lips were liquid with excess of paint. But Albert intervened.

"Price," he said, "is of no consequence here. It is true we provide slightly different service for varying fees and that there is a certain grandeur, a certain exaltation about a ceremony which is marked by additional touches of remembrance. We do not deny that survivors can demonstrate a deeper devotion, a more profound affection by indicating certain preferences in the matter of detail. Memories may be sweeter and mellower because of these things."

"How much can you afford to pay?" the girl asked, her kindness muffled somewhat by the gum.

"I have fifty dollars with me," Martin said and watched carefully Albert's reaction. It was hardly favorable; he took a deep breath of exasperation, stiffened again and narrowed his eyes. "I can get more," Martin added quickly.

"You are thinking of this . . . payment," Albert said slowly, "as supplementing what Father Roth has already promised?"

"Yes," Martin said. That way it would work out. Certainly his mother had a right to some help from the Church, some petty dividend on the hundreds of thin coins jingled into collections. "I'm paying Father Roth back later," he lied, snatching his pride about him again, determined neither to owe nor to give the appearance of owing.

"That was not the impression we received," Albert said. And added quickly, as Martin's head banked up to stare at him, "Not of course that we are in the habit of discussing monetary matters with the clergy or anyone else in excess of necessity. Particularly," he smiled sadly, "at such a time. I would suggest, young man," the epithet grated on Martin, "that you allow us to deal with the details as we see fit. You may be sure that the dear one for whom you grieve will be treated not only respectfully and devotedly but even with a certain amount of pageantry. Never going, of course, beyond the solemn nature of such a ceremony." Albert clasped his hands delicately at his breast, bowed his head and moved gracefully, flexibly toward a small door which led back under the stairs they had passed on the way in. "If you'll excuse me . . ." His voice sunk to a sepulchral quietness, and with a muted flourish of hands he was gone, the small door fitting noise-lessly into its frame, the soft-shoed feet whispering softly down the stairs. His manner blanketed the room for a moment, until Martin rebelled against it, turned to the girl and shouted out defiantly against the smell of flowers and fluids, against the atmosphere.

"Does he mean I can't have it," he shouted. "Is that what he means?"

"Not so loud," she said, the gum showing between the moist lips, caution wrinkling the eyes. "That won't get you anywhere with Albert," she said. "He's Murray's son." As though that explained the confidence, the stifling superiority.

"A lot he knows," Martin said, "talking about survivors." He looked darkly at the small door, boring his jealousy through it. He leaned over the desk, looking down at the thick hair, the painted face. The desk was lower, he thought, than Father Kirkman's—and he blinked the thought from his mind like a tear from the eye.

"What have they done with her?" he said. "What are they going to do—give her the cheapest, crummiest funeral they can rig up? Complete Funeral—$49.00. Is that it? They might as well put her into a sack."

"You'll make yourself sick," the girl said. "That's no way to act. You mother'll be all right."

"They think they can talk you out of anything, these guys," he snorted away from the desk toward the wall, face to face with a calendar, decorated with an elaborate tombstone. The print read: "J. T. Murray's Sons—Your Friend in Need." The mortician obligingly ticked off the days for you, blocking in the black figures that indicated how much time to go. "This priest," he turned back and snarled at the girl, "bringing in a charity case, I guess. Full of sympathy and kindness. It won't cost him anything."

"It won't be the cheapest," the girl said. "If Albert took your fifty dollars, it would have to be the cheapest. If he holds out, he can get more through the priest. This is a business."

"How high do the big ones come?" he wanted to know.

"Anywhere," she said. "Three hundred. Five hundred. More than you've got. We checked you up."

The world estimated you, like a man pricing an automobile, judging value from appearance, manner, position. For his mother, there had been neither credit nor cash for a long time. You were weighed in a scale opposite a mass of gold and silver; if you were a Lynn, the coin won out, turning the balance.

"My fifty can help, can't it? I'll get more. I promise."

"If you had it now, it might mean something—" She looked at him with kindness. He was aware of her suddenly as a woman, his heightened emotions seeking outlet; the wide nostrils, the thick lips, the white of her throat showing palely against the black dress. Her blowziness itself incited desire. He remembered the psychiatrist brooding at him with disapproval and a suggestion of distaste. Another refusal; another denial; he'd be free of that, too, before long. How many things can the mind hold at one time, he thought, and struggled as though a high wave were beating down at him, threatening to wrestle him under the weight of gagging water. This girl was fat, he told himself; fat and untidy.

She was still talking. "It won't seem so bad tomorrow," her voice tried to intimate sympathy, glassily revealing her insincerity. "You let Father Roth handle it."

"Father Roth," he echoed. "I'll handle it myself. I don't need a priest." He flung open the small door and was inside, on the dark steps leading to the basement before she could move or even shout. He heard her high, hard voice beyond the door saying "Wait a minute!" as he went swiftly down three or four steps. Then the quiet assailed him, the quiet and the dark and he paused for a moment in a kind of fear, trying to explain to himself where he was going, trying to remind himself of what he might see in the dark regions at the foot of the bare wooden stairs. The girl opened the door behind him then and said: "You don't want to go down there,"—a note of horror in her voice— and he fled, thudding his feet on the wood, fled to the foot of the stairs and turned off to the right into a kind of alcove which was in utter darkness. He stood quietly for a moment, watching over his shoulder the shaft of strong light which fell slantwise on the steps from above, stood and waited. The girl mumbled something with an air of resignation and the swath of light telescoped, the door banged shut and he was in blackness.

He guessed she had decided to abandon him to Albert, who was presumably working away down here among the cadavers. The picture of Albert's precise and rhythmical mannerisms let loose on his mother enraged him, and he turned, and went past the foot of the stairs. But the darkness expunged all sense of direction and he had to stop and wait, fumbling out with his hand and finding, finally, the edge of the banister. Albert—he thought—Albert was certainly an opposing force, part of the amorphous "they" that occupied his resentment. Albert, going busily and gracefully about his ghoulish profession, chatting softly to widows and orphans, shrewdly sizing up the price of sorrow. He was another one, all right; a power; the day held no terrors for him.

His eyes focused in the gloom and revealed a slit of brilliance spraying out under a door ahead to his right. He fumbled toward it. The odor of chemicals was more acute now, and seemed to increase in pungence as he moved toward the light. He could hear a low hum beyond the door: Albert cheerily discharging his tasks. Resentment boiled in him again, spluttering along the edges of his brain, asking for action. Once unleashed, how far could anger go? It occurred to him frightfully that beyond Father Kirkman, beyond Albert, always another smirking face would appear crying to be struck down; the quest of the final face would be long, would be endless, with the "powers," the others, constantly increasing, propagating themselves efficiently. Nevertheless, he thought, you could strike it where you saw it, could pursue injustice as far as the fire of anger lit the way, follow the dancing shadows as long as their substances were within reach.

He was at the door now, and vaguely a sting in his palm conveyed to his brain the fact that his nails were being driven into his hands. He unclenched them in the half-light and held them up in front of him and flexed them, as though testing them; inspection before the attack, before the act. He was aware of perspiration along his forehead again, like the tide of passion, a fringe of the force to follow.

THE THOUGHT

He could hear the humming more distinctly now, although he had the impression that Albert was not immediately beyond the door, but farther away, inside still another room. Here below the surface of the ground, among the acrid odors and the tumbling to decay, was an appropriate place to throttle a man into agreement. He wondered grimly how Albert's glib pronouncements would sound with fingers hooked around his throat.

His hand was on the door when he remembered with a shock that he might see his mother beyond the door, view her in some obscene stage of the embalming process which might color his memories forever. He wasn't sure exactly what the process consisted in—he had vague images of Albert inserting giant hypodermic needles into the flesh of the arm and squeezing huge syringes, his mother's old body quaking and discoloring under the interior flood. But his new stubbornness won out, supported the hand on the door and helped him push in, tremblingly; no matter what fright awaited him, what unsightliness was revealed, it was no part of him to stop now; the debt they all owed his mother's memory was more important than any chance indignity to her fragile remains; her dignity as a person outweighed whatever accidental horror he might himself encounter. She must be honored; justice must be served.

He advanced into the room deliberately, doggedly, straining against his own impulses, which urged him back like the grip of hands. He repeated to himself his reasons, the necessity, repeated it again and again and propelled himself into the room as though advancing hand over hand along a taut rope against a prodigious resistance which tugged him back. Sheer power of will conveyed him, justified him, sustained him until he had gone some three or four steps across the sill, had accomplished what every cell of his body screamingly resisted. But the sigh of triumph to which his resolution might have been entitled caught bonily in his throat at what he saw.

Stretched on a slab before him, divested of clothing, gray and puckered, of sickening shade and texture, lay the weird collection of skin and shape that had once been Father Kirkman. He wondered afterwards what lingering trait identified it for him, for certainly there was little to relate the hulk to the man he had seen—seen and murdered—the night before. The skin, which was not the color of skin at all, but a transparent paleness through which lividity seemed to glow, gave the impression that it did not fit the structure assembled inside it; like a sack in which the burden has distributed itself crazily under the heft of mishandling. The face, fully revealed to him as the head sagged perceptibly toward the right—had it not been upright when he first saw it?—had not even the reality, the reassurance of a face done in dirty stone. It was devoid of anything, even the machinations of an artist, limp, blank, a caricature of expressionlessness. The lips were fixed firmly together only not quite accurately so that the bottom one slightly overlapped the upper, imparting to the features a sense of imbalance, of an insanity which had not so much outlasted as succeeded the soul in tenancy.

It was as though a laugh had been perverted, turned inside out to reveal the hems and stitches and empty ugliness of the lining; it was a joke gone lewdly wrong.

114

The eyes, of course, were open with an intensity that belied lashes; were open and staring at him in a parody of seeing; not with accusation, which would have been expected and therefore a relief, a sanity among the horror, but blindly, bottomlessly, as though some insect-like being were staring gleefully at him from the other end of a thin, narrow tunnel which admitted only the eyes and therefore must concentrate all the diabolical perversity of a nothingness into the one outlet. The eyes appeared to be pointed directly at him with the intensity and meaninglessness—a simultaneous presence and absence—of two zeros. The horror consisted in his beholding a negation, a lack, where once there had been something; and though the externals, the members and gestures of the body were intact, the source and core of life had been withdrawn, the vitality descanted by some trickery which left the vessel itself upright. The blood and the beat of the body had departed, leaving behind innumerable and ineradicable memories, and to Martin Lynn the enormity of the blankness, this horror of nothing, presented itself because it was he who had removed the blood, the beat, had battered them out in blind fury so many wobbling years ago when he was younger than his sin now made him and his own blood rushed and swirled and stormed inside his head.

Glass clinked against glass somewhere and he heard a humming, a satisfied, unaware humming which vibrated breezily in this mausoleum of the soul. Albert, he remembered fuzzily, and was amazed that he could ever again attach a name to anything, could distinguish an identity out of the endless spaces, could anchor any noise to any source.

"Forgive me," he said to the heap of discolored nothingness on the slab, and did not recognize his own voice and for a surprised second, split between one awareness and the next, the syllables startled him and he withdrew toward the door, walking backwards, his hands groping in the chill air for the door frame. Panic whipped him then, panic and exhaustion of the spirit assailed him at the same time and as he turned to run he was afflicted with an unutterable weariness, akin to the result of running for miles and miles over plain, flat, unmarked country where progress was impossible to calculate; so that where the panic lashed him on, fatigue dragged him back and the same contest of nerve against nerve, of muscle against muscle which had slowed his advance to the corpse now marked his retreat. The humming advanced toward him like a drum. But at last he was out the door and fleeing through darkness, stumbling and falling against the stairs, and picking himself up and pounding his feet on the steps and thudding against the door at the top of the passageway. His hands clawed the surface and found no knob so that he beat his fists against it finally and cried out in the darkness and sobbed. At the ghosts of Father Kirkman and his mother, the spectre of his own sin, and his callousness and his weakness all at once, weeping for every corner of his being in a welter of tears. And then his quaking hand found the knob and the touch of the metal steadied him in an indescribable manner and he became calm with a terrible coldness and seemed to feel nothing. He turned the knob and cast the weight of the door away from him and stood looking into the small office, at the impassive calendar on the wall and the untidy girl at the desk who was looking at him in wide-eyed dismay and at a priest who sat opposite her and who was young and turned his face also toward the door with a look of rather mild surprise in which concern was mingled. Martin tried to smile, to speak, to gesture—to do something to indicate that there was no connection between himself as he stood there and the sobbing maniac who had been leaning against the door a moment ago, but out of the shaken inventory of his mind, no appropriate move presented itself, and he only stood.

Albert's voice behind him broke the silence, Albert speaking as his soft shoes rattled a muted tattoo of regularity on the steps as he ascended. "Whatever was all that racket?" he said, with a kind of feminine shock in his voice. Martin moved slowly, weakly up into the room and stood beside the door, leaning against the wall, to clear the way for Albert, who came in turn up the steps and stood in the doorway with his hands on his hips and his head slanted questioningly to one side. "I couldn't possibly imagine—" then he saw the priest and the high-pitched annoyance which he had adopted to express his indignation gave way to a tone of respect, mingled with lingering overtones of his exasperation. "Father Roth," he said, "did you hear——?"

"Are you all right?" the girl asked, leaning across the desk toward Martin; and he thought how nice it was of her to ask; how nice of her to stop chewing her gum just a moment and ask about him, so that he almost smiled except that his lips trembled too much to shape it properly. The priest rose then and came over to him, with solicitude in his young eyes and his hands outstretched, but the boy saw suddenly the crucifix in the hand and the hand upraising, going back and back and back before it descended, and he collapsed headlong on the cool linoleum of the office and thought, in a brief strip of clarity, that this time he would really go insane, this time surely the veil could be dropped, like a blanket, over his head, and he would be spared the memory of the murder, of the pride, of the determination. This time surely his mind would mercifully crack and dissolve and scatter his consciousness into oblivion and he would be free of the past. And while he wished for it painfully, he began to black out and was aware for the merest pinpoint of consciousness— just before the curtain came down—that he was still sane, that reality still bore relentlessly in on his soul and it was only his body that had succumbed.

VII

Everything rearranged itself, as he had known it would; all the hateful details reappeared. The priest first of all, his face coming slowly into focus above the Roman collar like a pink worried cherub and then beyond the face, which was very close to his own, the ceiling of the room which was painted a clean, sharp gray. Then as he moved his head, the girl and Albert and the top of the door and the calendar and the linoleum which turned out to be a neat brown with a simple design. It developed that the priest was kneeling on the floor beside him and then there was a splash of water against his lips and his teeth clattered against glass and he was drinking.

"I have no idea," Albert was saying, his voice coming

and going, fluctuating like a badly-tuned radio announcer. "I didn't even see him." The girl said. "I couldn't stop him. He started down—" and the priest said "Do you want any more?" and the voice was clear and even, so he shook his head.

"Thank heaven he's conscious," Albert said, casting his eyes up, his hands describing his relief in the air. "He's certainly a very extreme case; no doubt some morbid attachment existed between him and his mother——"

"Please," the priest interrupted. "Is there a bed upstairs? We'd better make him comfortable for a while."

"No," Martin spoke as though his lips were swollen and he reached a hand up toward his face to feel if this was true. "I—I'm all right," he said, and felt a prodigious pain in his head. He was still himself; he could not leave his body, could not convert his eyes into expressionless targets; he could not escape. There was a drumming in his brain, too, a drumming he had survived; it was the old man beating his feet against the slab in an impossible tattoo.

He tried to get up then, and Albert and the priest helped him to his feet, supported him over to the chair and let him down easily onto the seat. He tried to concoct explanations, excuses for his behavior, summoning up reasons hazily in the whirl of his brain, formulating half-sentences of apology which he could never seem to finish. But a numbness grew over him like a film and he found he could only sit in the chair and stare back into the sightless eyes which pursued him now, superimposing that strange hollowness which he could distinguish only as mirth over whatever he looked at. The priest was talking and Albert was talking but the conversation seemed suspended on wires above his head, passing him by, entirely incomprehensible, and all his attention was drawn to the eyes which were always directly opposite his own— as though they were attached to his forehead, dangling from a support which was fastened to him, as boys used to fasten meat on a stick extended over a dog's nose, so that the animal became both the tempter and the tempted at the same time. He found it difficult even to recall where he had met the eyes before, or in what connection; they were familiar somehow. But above all, they were there, opposite him, with that queer sense, not of boring in at him, but of boring away from him, like endless telescopes through which he was doomed to peer forever, seeing nothing.

"Grief," Albert was saying, and the words drifted as through smoke. "It often takes hold this way," he said, and his head was bobbing out the exaggerated effeminate inflections. "Father, you wouldn't believe some of the things we see here. People have absolutely no control, no control at all. Some of them, that is. It depends so much on training, education, family——"

Martin found himself breaking in. "You wouldn't know," Martin said. "You've probably never loved anybody. You don't know what it does." Albert looked at him with damp comprehension, saying "There," and shaking his head. "There, there."

"You don't know," Martin said again, weakly, and bowed his head and shoulders down and dug his fingers into his head and wondered why he had spoken at all.

That did no good; you could talk yourself blue in the face before they'd listen. The question was, what was his next move? Should he continue the masquerade, carry out his pretense of being crazed by grief? He could relieve his anxiety, close the eyes forever perhaps, by telling the young priest here what he had done, by recounting the whole story detail by detail. "Bless me, Father, for I have sinned . . . I killed a man." Craftily he remembered that he could confess the bare fact, without elaboration, devoid of illumination; that he could carry away from the young priest forgiveness and freedom without actually divulging the circumstances. It would be a good joke; it would be using their own methods on them; deceit and trickery: the letter of the law divorced from the spirit.

The priest said: "Would you like to go home now?" and Martin looked up into his face. It was unbelievably young; the last few hours had erased all memories of young priests; he had thought that they were all old and gray, old and gray and pop-eyed and dead. But no matter how young they were, he wasn't going home; not yet. He'd come here for something.

"I want to know about my mother," he said and heard his voice speak low-pitched and tremulous and breathlessly. "I came here to see she had—a decent funeral."

"Of course she'll have a decent funeral," the young priest said. "That goes without saying. You musn't worry about that."

"I got money," Martin said. "If it's a question of money." He fumbled in his pockets for the bill, found it and tossed it on the floor at Albert's feet, where it unwadded itself partly and lay like a large and even-sided leaf. "There's the money," he told them, looking defiantly up at the young priest. "I want her taken care of right."

"We've fixed that, son," the young priest said. Son, Martin thought; he's barely older than I am; he looks like a baby. They were always stepping up on things and looking down on you.

"You fixed it," he said with disgust. "You wouldn't fix anything, you priests. I asked that—" and he stopped abruptly, the words freezing on his tongue. Had he said too much? Would they be able to tell from that? It never before occurred to him that he might reveal himself; that the errant words might come unwarily from his own lips, betrayal in a position of the mouth. "Take the money," he said loudly, hoping the violence of voice would conceal his previous thought. He pointed at it, looked at Albert. "Take it up," he said, and rose to his feet, swaying somewhat. "She's got to have the best, that's all," he was almost screaming. "She was a good woman."

And then he stood wildly, saying nothing, afraid of words suddenly, afraid the flood of language might wash up phrases that he dare not use. Albert stood firm-lipped, disapproval showing in the prim lines around the mouth.

The young priest bent over and plucked the money from the smooth floor, and held it out to him, barely looking at it. "Take it," the young priest said, gently.

"I don't want it," Martin said brokenly. "It's for my mother. Why do you think I've done all this?"

"For love," the priest said promptly. "I'd do the same for my mother. It's perfectly understandable. We do not always see what God's getting at in the things He does.

122

We think death is a punishment for us; but it's only a trial, only a short time. You keep this," he pushed the bill into Martin's limp hand, "and let me see to it that your mother is taken care of."

It would be only right, Martin thought, for them to do it. In a way his mother's death was their responsibility anyway. They were the ones that had chained her down, fixed on her the heavy manacles of a belief that exalted poverty; they had taught her resignation and patience and the tail between the legs. But the tyranny of charity would strengthen their position, would make him dependent again, oil once more the wheels of obedience in the old groove. It would contest his new position, question the advantage he had gained, throw him back again into his role of subservience. These priests wanted to run everything. He jerked his hand away from the money and stepped back.

"I can have her taken somewhere else, you know," he told them, ranging himself against the three of them. "It isn't as if I haven't got money. You think I'm poor, all of you. You think you can shove me around. But I know my rights." He didn't want to carry it too far, didn't want to tempt them too much. They might, of course, take him at his word. Albert might snatch at the opportunity to be rid of a charity case. He remembered that he hadn't seen his mother in the gloomy cellar with its bitter atmosphere, and it dawned awkwardly on him that his mother and Father Kirkman lay below together, sharing the insensibility of death, stretched out one beside the other, equalized at last among the chemicals.

"Excuse me, Father," the mild voice crept in from the

hallway, which was behind him, and he spun around to face its owner. A man stood in the doorway, tall, clumsy, apologetic. "I walked right in. I thought it was usual." It was the detective from the theatre lobby. Martin wondered if he had been followed.

"Mr. Mandel," the young priest said, and there was relief in his tone. "I didn't mean to keep you waiting so long——"

Mandel looked at Martin calmly for a moment, then his gaze drifted away, as he bowed his head. "This young man," he inclined his head vaguely, "looks upset. Anything wrong?"

"Nothing really," the young priest said. "He's—troubled, that's all. I think we'd better take him home."

Like an invalid, Martin thought; or a moron. Poor, poor Martin Lynn, they were saying to themselves, pigeon-holing him in their minds, marking him. But he had neither the strength nor the courage to protest. The priest pressed the money into his hand and he accepted it, pocketed it, wearily, trying to recall all that had happened and in what order. The eyes were with him again, staring.

"Monday for the funeral, then," the young priest was saying. "If there's anything further . . ." Albert buzzed away busily, his head pecking at the details, the arrangements. The girl edged back to her desk and sat down, her gum slapping against her lips. The detective lounged in the doorway, looking off into space.

The priest and the policeman, Martin thought; popping up everywhere. If they had known he was a murderer, a sinner, they couldn't have been more persistent. The priest had been at his home the night his mother died, the cops in the diner, this spare, absent-minded man clomping up the lobby of the movie house. They were all over the place. They never let you sleep, Craig had said, and he had not even been speaking of the priests. He thought he must leave town after all this was over, go away some place where his entire history didn't edit every passing glance.

The priest took his arm then and guided him out through the hall and he went along, passively, thinking he had better submit, had better encourage the belief that he was crazed with grief, the sorrowing son gone berserk. The detective stumped along behind them, padding on the carpeted hall.

"Feeling better?" the priest asked as they came out into the air. And he was. He breathed deeply and was aware of the sharp clear fragrance of the autumn morning and the intense ordinariness of the street: the passing cars, the clean stone steps, a group of boys yelling, off somewhere. He thought how sweet and calm the day might be if he were burdened only with his mother's death. He imagined that he was coming out of Murray's with two friends, after having made the final arrangements about the funeral. They would be saying commonplace, comforting things to him, or discoursing eagerly of neutral topics to divert his mind: the young, open-faced priest and the laconic policeman, coming down the steps beside him in friendliness.

But the reality was different. They were his enemies, both of them, traveling on different but parallel levels in pursuit of him. He had broken laws which both had dedicated their lives to preserving. It would be more ac-

curate to imagine that he was under arrest, that the policeman was holding his arm instead of the priest, and that it
was the priest and not the policeman who came behind
them, murmuring prayers for his soul. If they only knew,
he said to himself, they'd be surprised. That would give
them a shock. It might make them look around more carefully the next time they saw a boy like him. If they knew
why he was really upset, as they called it—troubled.

The car was a police car, parked with its privileges
between green signs which kept clear the area before the
entrance to the funeral home. It was lettered and num-
bered, identified as official no matter what angle you
viewed it from. He had a sudden impulse to run, but it
was dispelled before he could clearly formulate it, and
the policeman was opening the door, gesturing him into
the back seat.

"In we go," the priest said briskly, a smile darting across
his face. It was what a friend might have said, Martin
thought—and climbed in thinking that he had no friends
who would treat him with such solicitude, such consideration; nobody to say sincerely that they were sorry for his
trouble and anything they could do . . . he was all alone
now; there was nobody anywhere he could turn to. Nobody really; Mrs. Lally was no substitute for friendship,
for affection.

He sat weakly on the back seat, while the priest and
the detective sat side by side in front like footmen.

"It's like you were arresting me," he said suddenly, the
thought finding its own simple words and leaping out.
The detective half-turned his head; the priest swung his
shoulders around and smiled at him.

"You need rest," the priest said. "Rest. And I'll bet you haven't eaten this morning." Martin hadn't.

"Arresting you," the detective said wryly as he started up the motor. "That's an odd thought. Arresting you for what?"

Perhaps, Martin thought, it was a trap, after all. Had they known he ran? Had someone seen him startle and flee from the shell of the old priest?

"Anything," he said, vaguely. "Anything at all. I'm sorry I made a spectacle."

"It's nothing," the priest said. "Don't think about it any more. Everything's going to be all right."

The aphorism again, the phrase grinding over and over again, applied to any situation, like the commandments, the cautions, the don'ts.

"She's got to have a good funeral," he said monotonously, clinging to his purpose, exhibiting it for their inspection, putting forward his claim to virtue. "That guy in there; he didn't want to do it."

"He didn't understand," the young priest said, "and maybe you didn't quite make yourself clear. You see, I had your mother taken here—last night. The lady next door suggested it. I hope it's not against your wishes."

They churned along a side street lined with pushcarts and buyers. Martin remembered it was Saturday, Saturday about noon, somewhere in there. The long history had taken place within the last fifteen hours. That was all. He shuddered as the eyes impinged upon him again, materializing in the air of the automobile, obscuring his view of the priest and the detective. And the film started up again; the reenactment of last night: all the sickening details retraced again, performing just for him.

"I know we can give your mother a fine funeral," the young priest was saying. His face was profile to Martin now; he looked out across the detective. "Yesterday it might not have been possible, but last night, a friend of mine died. He left some money for just such a purpose. It was an old priest."

Martin's hands dug into the upholstery, searching for a grip on something, a solidity somewhere.

"Isn't that right?" the young priest was asking the detective.

"That's what the lawyers said," the detective answered.

And Martin thought he would laugh; felt tingles of hysteria sparking up at the back of his throat. He had said to the darkened apartment "It's all worked out." He hadn't known then how well. The murder had provided for his mother's funeral; good coming stubbornly and ridiculously out of evil.

The voice went on over the hum and blur of traffic, drifting across to him from the front seat. "An old priest named Father Kirkman. He was killed—by somebody—somebody who didn't know him."

They were at the rectory suddenly, before he knew it, the streets flashing by while he nursed his distraction in the back seat, and the priest was getting out.

"There's so much to do," the young priest was saying, as he climbed out on the pavement.

"Want to come up here with me?" Mandel said. He didn't turn his head. Martin could see the straight-set hat, the narrow hedge of the shoulders; the presence of the quiet detective was like a sullenness in the air; the gray brooding before the storm.

"I'll get out here, too," he said. "I don't live far away."

The priest looked sharply at him. "Mr. Mandel can drive you," he said. "You don't want to take a chance on being sick."

"I'm fine," Martin mumbled, and pushed the handle. It was an obvious trap. He and the detective alone in the police car. A few casual, indirect questions; he couldn't trust himself, couldn't leave himself open to the temptation. There are other occasions besides sin, he thought. There are occasions of good, too. As he poked his head outside the car, the church loomed up before him, vacant and staring at mid-day: like the funeral home, he thought. But it provided an excuse, an excuse that was also an exhibition; it would produce an impression. "I thought I'd say a prayer," he looked at the church as he said it, not daring to meet their eyes.

"If you want," Mandel said, and stared through the window-glass at him, smilingly. "Say one for me. I got a tough case. St. Jude, isn't it?"

"That will help more than anything," the priest said. The car whirred away, purring officially off down the quiet street.

"You'll find it quiet there," the priest said, standing at the curb in the sun and looking toward the church; it was of red brick and built awkwardly, with unexpected slantings and too many square corners. "Maybe it'll give you—peace." Now would come the old, tattered words, the boy thought; priests reeled them off like tape out of a machine, automatically, streaming foolishly into the wastebaskets, meaning nothing.

"Blessed are they that mourn," the priest said, "for they shall be comforted." He looked uncomfortable himself, standing there in his black clothes, with the white collar like a band below the cherubic face. It chained him to fear, Martin thought, to superstition, to the magic words which frightened you into obedience. If only the red-haired priest would go, go into the rectory, go up the curved steps through the hateful door, it would provide escape; he wouldn't have to go into the church after all. Why had he said it? There was no need.

But the priest didn't go. "We have both lost—someone we loved," the young priest said, and put a hand on Martin's shoulders. The boy shuddered beneath the clasp; like the detective in the diner, he thought. Couldn't they keep their hands off?

"It's a difficult time." He would have an answer, Martin thought, remembering the glib phrases in the catechism, the penny lovelorn column where all the answers were pat. Always the catch in the throat was classified, the stone in the breast weighed lightly in the balance of the stock phrase. Nobody knew—except himself—about love, the thin figure of his mother flagging across his mind. He pulled away from the hand and flung himself up the stone steps, accepting any sanctuary in preference to the old, enslaving forces and as he went he breathed a sudden, inexplicable prayer to be fully free of the ancient practices, free of the pasts and his fears. He stopped praying abruptly as he entered the church.

VIII

Craig saw the two detectives moving among the restaurant tables, and guessed they were coming toward him. He congratulated himself that he had chosen this cheap place; it would fit snugly with his denials, his hurt protestations of innocence. He stirred his coffee and smiled at them.

"Well, gentlemen," he said cheerily. "A pleasant surprise. Won't you join me? Or were you going to anyway?"

They pulled out chairs and sat down heavily. "The food is inexpensive but nourishing," he smirked at them. "Hardly enough to keep you two at your present weight, but adequate." They leaned on the table, forward toward him, like twins, their bulks blotting out the chairs, dwarfing the table. "What is it this time? I haven't been keeping up with the police news. I confine myself to the want ads these days." He held the smile spread across his face banteringly. It was a role they were familiar with.

"Just a couple of questions," one of them said methodically. "We're interested in how you're getting along," the other said, giving his companion a glance of caution. "We haven't talked to you on business for a long time, Craig."

"I've missed you, gentlemen," Craig smiled at them. "Honestly I have. My story is a simple one, typical of many bright young men in these parlous days. It's only recently that I've returned to civilian life and I am even now trying to pick up the threads of my blighted career."

"That's what we want to know," the first said. "About your career. About your career last night, for instance."

"You wrong me," he told them. "You are familiar with

131

the army's undoubted capacity for restoring honor and reputation to wayward citizens. I am happy to say their methods were successful with me, if I may report it modestly. I am a new man—in fact, a man. I was made a man by the army. If your questions have to do with your usual inquiries into illegal activity, I, gentlemen, am not your man."

"Always talking," the first one said.

"Wait a minute," said the second. He planted his blunt hands flat on the table. "What are you doing now, Craig? You working?"

"Unfortunately, no." Craig continued to smile. "My regeneration has not yet progressed to such fearsome lengths. I am looking for a suitable position. If you know of any——"

"How long you been out?" the second one pursued.

"Two months," Craig said. "I refresh myself on vital statistics for just such occasions. A man's past keeps popping up. You policemen forget the face of the world has changed; universal catastrophe. Even weak characters like myself are not immune."

"You fixed for money?"

"A pittance," Craig said, musingly. "I think that old-world expression describes it best. Government bounty. Rehabilitation remuneration, shall we say?"

"Twenty bucks a week for you?" the first one said.

"It is hardly ample," Craig told him. His gesture included the restaurant. "You see yourselves I am not eating in the style from which you used to discourage me."

The excitable one grunted disbelief. The grim one said: "Not like the old days, is it? We used to tip our hats when

132

we questioned you, out of politeness to your many lady friends."

"The army counsels celibacy," Craig said with a simulation of sorrow. "I was a model soldier." The excitable one snorted.

"Here's the pitch," the grim one said. "Last night the Galaxy Theatre was held up. The cashier got shot. One of our men on the beat saw you in the neighborhood. Remembered you from the old days. We're taking you in on suspicion."

"My, my," Craig said, holding his coffee cup delicately. "How much did I get?"

"You tell us!" the excitable one said.

"A movie," Craig thought about it. "One thousand? Fifteen hundred? Hardly worth my while."

"Even so, you better come along," the grim one told him. They sat like fat vultures across the table. "May I finish my coffee?" Craig asked. "My digestion is not so hardy as it once was."

"Your digestion was always good," the excitable one said. "You could always drink. Even after Martin Lynn took his leap."

Craig set the white cup deliberately onto the saucer. "Martin Lynn," he said, and managed a trace of guiltiness. "Strange you should mention him. Today of all days." He let his gaze linger over their heads, drawing a mask of reminiscence over his features.

"Why is it strange?" the grim one looked at him expressionlessly.

Craig seemed to recall himself with an effort. "You think I'd tell you? You believe that about the sins of the father,

133

don't you? A private memory, gentlemen." He noted with satisfaction that they exchanged a glance. "One returns to find many echoes."

"Do you know his kid?" the excitable one asked eagerly.

Craig raised his eyebrows, took time to light a cigarette, blew smoke carefully into the silence. "Whose?" he said, as though he didn't really know.

"Never mind," the grim one muttered.

"Lynn's, you mean," Craig spoke it easily, as though he were lying. "A fine boy. I remember him. Like his father. So much like his father." He watched the effect on them, purring the words at them gently. "Environment is so strong." He pretended to shift the subject purposely. "Look at me, for instance."

They continued to stare at him for a moment. "Let's go," one of them said. "You're finished."

"These formalities take so much time," Craig murmured and rose to his feet. They lumbered behind him among the tables. It had been comparatively simple, he thought and smiled winningly at the cashier as he paid his check.

IX

When the bell rang, the girl expected it would be Malcolm, and the prospect refreshed her. His airiness would distract her, lead her out of the world of worry into reality. Since she had left the rectory, uneasiness had plucked at her.

In the street, a garrulous old woman, the perfect prototype of the parish gossip, complete with atrocious hat and long neck, had accosted her with loud sympathy for her uncle's death. "A terrible shock to us all," she remembered the voice, croaking away on the quiet street. "Why, he seemed like the Church itself to me, Father Kirkman did. Such a good man." The woman had inclined her head to the side and blinked repeatedly, patting her hand. "We feel for you, dear," and assumed a gait of mourning, carrying her fat fund of sympathy before her like her block of a handbag, like a defense, as she moved away rapidly.

She had been no help. There was, the girl thought, nothing that mattered less to her than her uncle. Certainly no honest sorrow wept in her; only this faint illusion of pain which had a blunted edge. At the apartment, she found herself picking up small objects and putting them down again, rearranging Mary Jane's inevitable flowers. She directed her attention to two different books without success. Something flashed warning inside her, a light unidentifiable through a mist. Only a faint measure of anger was discernible—anger at the impudent detective who had hinted accusation. And yet that was routine, she told herself—the typical method of the blundering official, turning over every stone, asserting authority among the cowering who were his usual quarry. Reduced to cold facts, this remained: her uncle was dead—if violently was no concern of hers—the marriage was postponed. This was intermission merely, the time of waiting which the stupid convention demanded.

She smoothed her hair before the hall mirror and let the doorbell sound again before she went to relieve it, presenting a slickness to Malcolm which was her real self.

But the figure that hunched and gave a momentary impression of dangling in the hallway was not Malcolm's. It was Mandel the detective instead.

"You'll excuse me," he said. "I want to talk some more."

She displayed her annoyance, in her face, in the unwilling resignation of her voice. "Again," she pronounced it coldly. "I suppose you must come in." He ambled in long strides down the hall to the feminine front room, sat down awkwardly among the conflict in furnishing which distinguished her taste from Mary Jane's.

"I hope you haven't come to insult me," she held the advantage her tears had given her some hours before.

"Not that," he said, his head bowed, eyes on the floor, his long arms extending down beside him. The hands almost touched the floor. "I need help, that's what."

She had assumed somehow that the police went through a ritual series of movements, checking charts, comparing fingerprints, putting through long-distance calls—she had watched keen-eyed men riffling through filing cases in the rotogravure sections. It had all appeared entirely impersonal: the criminal surrendering finally to the system, brought to earth by the inexorability of efficiency. But somewhere in the city, walking the streets, smoking cigarettes, looking nervously behind him, moved the man who had murdered her uncle; it was a new, disconcerting thought.

"I got nothing to go on," Mandel told her mournfully, staring at Mary Jane's geranium pots, at her own neatly-spaced prints on the wall. "A man is murdered. No reason anywhere. No weapon. Nobody sees anybody. The housekeeper's off for the night. The sexton is up in the steeple

someplace and when he comes down he doesn't see anybody either. I'm chasing a ghost."

He was a pitiable figure, sprawling in the chair, droning
away in his calm, dead voice. She waited for him to go
on. Did it matter if the man was never found?

"I want two things," he said, staring hazily at Mary
Jane's statue in the shadowed corner, running his vague
eye along the shelf of books. "First, I want you to think. Is
there anything connected with your family that might
help? Any—we don't call them feuds now—unpleasantness? Any scrambling for money, any old grudges?"

It was, of course, impossible. She could recall nothing
and, in any case, it seemed unlikely; the memory of her
mother was indistinct but highly respectable. She could
not imagine anyone hating her uncle—"except myself," she
told him in a small voice.

"That's one thing," he said, ignoring it. "Think back.
The other thing is maybe harder. People will be calling
you, expressing sympathy, sending things, all the stuff
people do to recognize death. Would you keep an eye out
for anything that suggests suspicion? It must be somebody
who knew him."

She reminded him that their worlds were not the same;
that her connection with her uncle was remote, unpubli-
cized—suppressed, she reminded herself. "He's just an old
priest," she had said uncomfortably to Malcolm the first
time her uncle had interfered with their lives. "Nobody
will call me," she said to Mandel.

"There's the funeral home," Mandel persisted, but in his
gentle, indirect way. "We're getting a break. Priests are
usually laid out in the church. Friends will come there,

putting in their last prayers, giving comfort to the bereaved. You have a right to be there all the time, to see who comes. I'm"—he looked with a kind of disconsolateness down his stringy frame—"conspicuous."

"You mean, stay there—with the body," she recoiled from the idea. It had always smacked of the barbaric to her; the living grouped ghoulishly around the recent dead, murmuring in the candlelight, the survivors recounting over and over again the history of the final hours. "I couldn't," she turned away from him in her chair.

"It may not help at all," he admitted with a kind of disappointment. "Just an idea. Then again it may." Incredulity suddenly sparked the noncommittal tones. "You do want to help find your uncle's murderer, don't you?" His inflection bordered on shock.

"I want him found," she said. "But still . . . to stand there smirking with his body. All the old women. That's who it'll be. One of them stopped me on the street today."

"There'll be others," he said. "You'd be surprised. Your uncle was known. I'll be there myself, unofficially. We were friends." He stared off comfortably at a memory. She thought: this tall, dangling Jew and the short, round priest; it was like inter-religious propaganda. Then: "The murderer will probably come. It was a friend of his. At least, somebody who knew him. I'm sure of that."

"But if there was no reason," she countered, giving herself time to think about his proposal. She could imagine the playful gleam in Malcolm's eye when she told him. "Prehistoric," she could hear him say, and phrase an irreverent comparison.

"I meant I don't see the reason," Mandel said. "There

has to be one. Only a maniac would go in there, bash the old man on the head without some—" he had almost said provocation, "—motive. That's always a possibility, of course. But we've got to eliminate down to it." He looked at her, his eyes shaded by what appeared to be shyness. "You'd have to be there tomorrow and Sunday both. Then at the funeral. It won't be easy; it never is. But out of your love for him——"

More than anything she resented the use of the word; as though love were a flexible emotion that could be stretched to cover any chance relationship: the man in the subway, the parish gossip, Mary Jane—himself, even. She had tended no love for her uncle; its seed had withered long ago, in her teens, before that even; long before he had become clear to her as a symbol of imprisonment, of restriction. "You're of Irish descent," he spoke mildly, as though it were a compliment she expected him to pay. "You people feel these things—like us."

She recognized it for an appeal, a common ground she shared with him, and she felt its power. Not as a persuasion, but as a weapon. It was an estimate of her actually; a challenge which he tossed casually on the carpet between them, a comparison of heritages, calling on her to pay some mysterious debt to immigrant ancestors. She hated him for it, and singled out additional repulsions—his deceptive, diffident manner, the calculated shyness, the aggressive Semitism. And there was another factor: her refusal might cast the vague glance of his suspicion on her. Perhaps this was the real test he was making; whether the killer could bear up at sight of the killed.

"If you think it'll help," her voice was strained with her own struggle, her resentment, "I'll do it."

"He'll be—what do you say—laid out by six this evening. At Murray's." He got up with a surprising agility, and hovered cloudily over her. "Do you know where it is?"

"I'll find it," she said, as though to make clear it was not in her usual orbit; placing herself outside the sanctified, habitual circle of Catholics.

"Watch them all," he said briefly, as though reciting prepared instructions. "Anybody at all who looks strange, let me know. Any little thing at all. Too much grief, not enough—he might betray himself in any number of ways. He might stay too long on the prie-dieu."

She was faintly surprised at the word which seemed so exclusively Catholic.

"Is it true," she asked levelly, "about the murderer always returning to the scene of the crime?"

He chuckled slightly. "This won't really be the scene," he said. "But I don't know. It's happened, I guess. That's why they say it. I guess if enough murderers hear about it, it'll suggest something to them. They'll think it's part of the routine. I hope so."

Mandel stood in the doorway. "You told me how you feel. I imagine you'll be able to keep a sharp eye out. You won't be complicated by—grief." He turned. "I'll let myself out." She heard the door close softly and felt about the detective as she had felt about the young priest; that he was a man who knew too much about her. She had displayed her rebellion before them and elicited the same kind of pitying, superior glance that her uncle had focused on her. It occurred to her that the old man's demands on

140

her were still current; he had emissaries in the world, survivors bent on maintaining the old order. The gray head
was still weaving back and forth somewhere, leaning over
her apostasy. Perhaps the murder had been in vain after
all and there was no freedom from his horrible, hovering
protection; replacements kept coming to the front. It was
as though her uncle had bequeathed her to these men, like
a prized but unmanageable possession. She decided to
call Malcolm so they could laugh together about the grimness of it.

X

The church was always darkened in the daytime, the
strictness of the parish budget plunging the tabernacle
into gloom. In the sanctuary a red light glowed like a spot
of blood; elsewhere the pillars stiffened up into obscurity,
the statues postured fruitlessly in the shadows. Martin
came fearfully down the aisle, his footsteps stirring hollow
echoes in the dome. Was the priest watching him from
the altar, he wondered? He remembered how they had
used to lurk at the door to the sacristy, peering out un-
seen at the congregation. He had better go through all
the conventional motions.

He genuflected stiffly halfway up the aisle and sidled
into a pew. He had not been in St. Stephen's or in any
church since his father's death, when his mother and he
had attended daily Mass furtively together for a while.
His father had not, of course, been buried from the church;
the margin for repentance in the plunge from the bridge
had been too brief for Father Kirkman to grant the benefit
of the doubt, and his mother had wept frequently over the

bloated body gone to rest in unconsecrated ground and dedicated herself to daily Mass in reparation. She had given way to tears regularly at the Canon of the Mass. "Remember, O Lord, Thy servants . . . who have gone before us with the sign of faith," she would read in her missal, her lips trembling over the words. ". . . grant, we pray thee, a place of refreshment, of light, and of peace," and then touch her forehead to the back of the pew in front of her and cry convulsively. His father had not gone to refreshment or light or peace; his soul tossed uncomfortably somewhere along the river bottom, jerking against the weeds. And the bell tinkled sweetly over the pews as Martin's mother wept silently and Martin looked at her with round eyes and felt inexpressibly sad, and turned toward the altar and glared at the old priest, who mumbled along the altar-rail dispensing the bread of life to the innocent tongues. His hate had begun there, born darkly in puzzlement at the contrast between the weeping woman and the oblivious old man who went about his mystifying duties as though nothing at all had happened. His mother, habituated to inexorability, had only prayed more fervently, staring filmily through her tears at the demeaning, pleading type on the page.

But Martin had refused to go finally, had taken advantage of his dropping out of school and going to work and used the circumstance as an excuse to forswear the Church as well. It was the occasion for more tears at first, and sometimes in the beginning, he would absent himself from the flat for an hour or so on Sunday morning to avoid unpleasantness, going not to Mass, but to the smoky room above Counihan's grocery store where a poker game kept continuous, intent session from Friday to Monday. He would sit staring over the cards hopelessly, telling himself grimly he was right, losing a few pennies among the stale beer and the cigar butts and the clatter of chips on the wooden table, grinning in bleak embarrassment when lasciviousness broke in among the laconic bets. His mother found out in time and looked at him in mute disappointment when he returned one morning with a specious version of the sermon he had not heard. After that, he had not even pretended. "You're disobeying," his mother had told him. "You'll go to hell," and he would say, softly, since anger never interrupted their placid acceptance of each other: "Father's in hell, isn't he?" She had let him go his own way thereafter, but he knew a large proportion of the prayers were now for him and he was vaguely disturbed at adding to her burden, at making hope harder for her to summon up.

Now he looked fiercely at the high vaulting over his head, at the bare table of the altar stripped after the morning's Mass, at the fuzz of lights burning before the statue of Mary, and told himself again he had pursued the only possible course. Their treatment of his mother had vindicated him. His father had been evil and had been denied burial; his mother had been good and would be granted only the minimum of everything, would be muttered over and whisked away and lowered groaningly into the ground with the most precipitate of services. The equation was clear to him; justice did not appear on each side. If his father had been wealthy, extenuating circumstances would have been found; if his mother had been wealthy, dignity and solemnity and pomp would see her off. Money was the difference. Money was refreshment and light and peace. Everything else was merely awkward Gothic type arranged neatly on the thin pages of the missal; a spurious document read over and over again in search of the hidden meaning which could never be revealed because it had never been present. Anyway, the account was squared now.

A dark figure bumbled down the aisle past him, going like a ghost toward the altar. With abrupt self-consciousness, he assumed an attitude of prayer, entwining his fingers in front of him on the thin shelf of wood. The figure was bent and old and he watched it with disdain as it crouched uncertainly at the rail under the red lamp. Sibilances crept down the gloom toward him; the old prayers were floating up again, creating echoes against the stone. He remembered all the prayers himself; they stuck in the mind like profanity. "O my God, I am heartily sorry,"— always the dependence, the sniveling, the inferiority, the subjugation. Always what somebody else wanted. Throw yourself on His mercy, the priest said. That was a laugh. I'll pray, he thought suddenly, glaring defiantly along the dim edifice. I'll ask for something. "Let me be smart," he said audibly, the guttural tones rumbling up the walls harshly. "Let me get out of this. They think they're gonna catch me, run me down, make me own up to it. Give me help to be smarter than they are. It doesn't matter now, anyway; he's dead."

He exulted in the effort. "That'll refresh me; that'll give me peace."

There was a movement among the shadows on the altar. A light had come on in the sacristy and in the glow flung out onto the steps he saw a priest ascending to the golden hut which housed God, fumbling with the door to the tabernacle, genuflecting. A sick-call, he thought; somebody was dying somewhere and the final nourishment was on its way. There was a click as the Host was enclosed. The figure turned and came down the altar steps, facing him; it was the young priest.

Fear struck through Martin suddenly as he thought that the comfort of this had been denied to his mother; he had interfered with the sequence, denied her a consolation she would have wished had she realized she was so close to death. "You'll be all right," he had told her grimly, as though his words would effect the cure. "The priest'll just scare you; he'll set you back. You just wait; you'll be all right." The young priest moved silently out of sight, the light flickered off, the old lady whined away at the rail, piling up whispers along the roof. Perhaps if he *had* called the priest for his mother, the other thing would not have happened; perhaps this denial was even more sinful than the murder itself; maybe the murder was a punishment for his remissness. He trembled in the half-light, pressing hands together and sharpening the knuckles. He had denied his mother the Last Sacraments, he had killed a priest —he had been guilty of omission and murder and sacrilege. The whispers from the dome raged down at him, like the souls of the damned murmuring among the flames; he fancied he could hear his mother wailing piteously through a wall of steam like wavering cellophane up from the hell to which he had consigned her, her bony arms outstretched across an infinite distance. The old priest was there too, poking his gray head round a crucifix, chanting maledictions at him, while suffering swayed in the background. It was another film, carrying on its shuttered, flickering life, unwinding doom at him; as indestructible as light.

A door banged; the shadows thickened around the plaster saints; the old lady at the altar began a screaming, high-pitched lamentation, half whisper, half groan. The echoes filtered down on him from above, creeping among the corners and angles of the architecture. To his right a board creaked like the snap of a whip or the crackle of a fire. He turned his head sharply and stared in frozen fascination at a confessional box, hulking like a dim, un-adorned triptych in the artificial twilight. Although his eyes could not distinguish the lettering clearly, he knew the name on the plate was Father Kirkman's; it was the one he had always occupied, mopping his brow and assigning penances on sultry Saturday nights, sliding the panels open to invite the secret horrors. Martin had made his first confession there, stumbling tonelessly among the abject phrases.

Now he caught his breath as the whispers banked and swirled around the alcove like insects; the ghosts of old sins hanging in the air round their own graveyard. The endless line of penitents had left their record like notches in the wood; he remembered the old priest's face, patient and uncomprehending through the grill, staring ahead, not looking at the sins extended for inspection. "How many times?" "Did you do it deliberately?" Was the fat, stooped figure crouching there now, waiting to forgive his own murderer? The panel slid back, inviting Martin. A weary cough rumbled out at him from somewhere; the old lady? the street outside? his own imagination? The whispers clustered over the box; the curtain shook; the shadows bunched and moved.

Somehow the old man had come back, had got up from the hearth and the blood and tottered along the stone paving to the church and had been hiding since last night in the confessional. It appeared incontrovertible; undeniable; a sure thing. And the priest waited now, like an animal in a cave, for the unwary sinner, holding absolution like a bait in his fat hand, ready to pounce on penitence. But it was not enough bait to attract him; they'd never get him in there again. Father Kirkman could wait forever. He wondered sharply if the old man were still bleeding; was he mopping away blood now instead of perspiration; sponging at it absently as he listened? There was no killing the thing, after all: the commandments, the accuser, the past, the demands and the submission. His eyes were riveted on the box now, and he tried by squinting to brush aside the blackness and see clearly. It waited always in the darkness, in one form or another, the emotionless face behind the grill, like a radiophoto in the newspapers, waiting with stolid confidence in its smug fortress.

Panic struck through him like a spear. His feet tripped against the kneeling bench, his hands slipped and clutched at the pew-back. Somehow he struggled into the aisle, scuffing his shoes wildly against the boards; he was afraid for a moment that his feet were caught, but he wrenched them free and stood breathlessly in the aisle. He had the momentary impression that a black-cassocked figure reached across at him from the confessional, snatching at his coat. "My God, My God!" he said and plunged toward the back of the church, falling up the aisle in a choking fog of hysteria, frantic to be away from the sedentary figure of the old priest in the box, from the whispers and the shadows and the pursuing thoughts.

As he came out the door it was like light breaking around him, a glow of sanity on the sidewalks, the opposite house fronts, the blessed commonplace of a woman dragging a child along the pavement. He leaned against the cold wall and bowed his head and panted, seeming to hear still the furtive noises and to see still the vivid images of the darkness. He feared the door would open behind, that his pursuer would come doggedly after him.

He stepped out from the building and hurried away down the street, following the same path he had taken immediately after the murder, walking rapidly and praying crazily to himself, not daring to look back. He knew desperately that even as his feet padded shakily along the stone, he was really leaving nothing behind him.

XI

"Is there anything else, gentlemen?" Craig asked, smiling in the light from the high, square windows, standing beside the rolltop desk.

"One thing," the grim detective said. "Just one more. Mandel wants to see you."

Craig widened his smile. "Not really. Mr. Mandel. It'll be a pleasure. Which way?"

"I'll take you," the excitable one said. "You follow me."

They churned along the lofty, dim corridors of the city hall, threading their way among clerks and citizens. Everyone seemed to be carrying papers; the documents of respectability neatly executed; the taxes paid, the birth registered, the title cleared. They were such willing enemies, Craig thought, so cooperative, narrowed properly into columns, filling in the official forms, careful to observe the niceties, minding their own business. But Mandel—he was a different story.

They had to wait until Mandel completed a phone call. Then the detective ushered him through a door with a white porcelain knob into an orderly room, where Mandel pointed up behind a flat table.

"Delighted," Craig began, as the door closed on the detective. He would have extended his hand but Mandel's mild eyes avoided him. "It's been three years," he added, maintaining the banter in his tone, keeping his guard up. "A lot has happened since then, Mr. Mandel."

"A lot of it," Mandel intoned dryly, "has happened in the last two days. Do you mind if we omit the social stuff?"

Craig sighed. "Always bluntness," he said sadly. "The single track of officialdom; no way stations to brighten the journey. However, before the small type sets in, I like your new office." It was, of course, similar to the old; the bald floors, the city map blanketing the wall-space, the file folders spread on the blotter. Mandel half-gestured toward a chair.

"For once," Mandel said, "we're not going to talk about you."

"Dull," Craig sat down. "But I shall endeavor to keep up my interest. If you're anxious about French police methods, I avoided all contact. There were other—entertainments."

Mandel stared moodily at the blotter. "Tell me about a

boy named Martin Lynn," Mandel said. "You knew his father?"

Craig lit a cigarette with deliberation. "Lynn," he breathed the word out in smoke. "Martin Lynn's dead. Five years ago."

"I know that," Mandel said. "I was in the precinct the night they found him. This is his son. You know he had a son."

"A son," Craig meditated. "Come to think of it, I saw him once or twice. Skinny and dotted with pimples. He was fifteen—fourteen, somewhere in there. We are not— intimates."

"Lynn's wife just died," Mandel distributed the information like dry crumbs.

"A shame," Craig said. "She couldn't have been so old."

"She was poor," Mandel said. "It wasn't age so much. Although they tell me she looked sixty. Worrying wears you down. Do you have a wife?"

Craig arched his eyebrows. "Had." Craig wadded meaning into it. "She left with a salesman. His product slips my mind at the moment. But it wasn't ice." Worry would never get her down, he appended a footnote in his mind. "Is young Lynn following what you conceive as his father's footsteps?"

"Or what you conceive," Mandel said. "You mentioned him, didn't you?" He nodded his head vaguely toward the right. "To the boys."

"You wrong me," Craig said, liking the phrase. It embodied his synthetic innocence, his safe badinage. "They brought him up. I refused to discuss him. It sounded like a frame."

Mandel stared out the window. "You don't believe in environment as a formative force?"

"Such a pedantic sentence," Craig mocked. "You can't expect a yes or no, Professor. It's a hem-and-haw question. If you mean do I look askance at young Martin Lynn because his father was a—what shall we say—miscreant—then I say: ridiculous." He blew more smoke into the air, brightened his tone. "My own father was a model citizen. Of course, the kid might have ideas of his own."

"Just the same," Mandel pursued, "Martin Lynn's son; he might be mad at somebody. He might feel cheated. If you were him, who would you be mad at?"

"What a question!" Craig laughed merrily. "The world, maybe. The police. A man who pushed me in a streetcar. A waiter who passed me up. Who wouldn't I be mad at?" He thought for a moment, then quietly: "The same people I'm mad at anyway."

Mandel drummed idly on the desk, his fuzzy blue eyes aimed at a corner of the room. "For once," Craig said, in a strained voice, the banter suddenly gone, "I'm willing to dispense with the formalities. Why all this? I don't know anything about this kid. I'm not the one to ask."

"Some funny things," Mandel said thoughtfully as though Craig had not spoken. "He's a quiet, orderly kid. No bad habits except a poker game now and then. All of a sudden things pile up." He swept his eyes up to Craig's face. "You took an army physical. What'd the psychiatrist say to you?"

Craig relaxed, disposed of the cigarette, sat back in the chair. "Mandel," he muttered reprovingly. "That's old stuff now. No more jokes there."

"I'm asking you," Mandel said, steel glinting beneath the soft voice, "an official question. You're under suspicion yourself, you know."

"Well," Craig straightened up, fitted the scornful smile across his lips. "I suppose I'll never quite get used to police methods. I thought we were having a chat . . . old times."

"They had the record on the boy," Mandel pursued. "4-F, psychoneurotic. But they were vague. It might be anything. Lack of cooperation. Anti-social. Perversion. Why this kid?" He looked again at Craig. "What did they say to you?"

Craig laughed. "They look at you with a leer and want to know about your sex life. I got a clean slate."

Mandel lined his brow with a question. "I talked to this kid. High-strung all right. Nervous. But nothing more. I mean, you wouldn't think so."

"Policemen are so naïve," Craig commented. And remembered the boy. And remembered also the scholarly man at the enlistment office who had looked him up and down and scribbled on a paper. "Look, Mandel. Here's what happens. If you tell 'em you've had no sexual experience, they take on as though you're—a murderer. Look at you as though you had no head. It's the new freedom; if you haven't taken advantage of it, they check you off queer. I saw it happen to a guy. After you're in the army, they give you prophylactics and tell you not to use them; but they insist on it before they let you in. I always had the feeling the psycho doctors were subsidized by a monopoly."

Mandel kneaded the information together between his

long hands. "So the boy might be all right and get marked 4-F for a queer. It might make him hate even more people."

Craig shrugged. "I supplied the facts. Diagnosis is your job."

"Okay, Craig," Mandel said absently.

Craig rose to his feet. "Is the inquisition over?"

"I guess it is," Mandel said. "Thanks. Thanks a lot."

"I seem to have been of help," Craig smiled his way to the door. "I hope this medical advice won't brand me an informer back at the precinct. After all, with conditions as they are, I may have to resume my prewar habits any day now. I wouldn't want them to lose faith."

"Not an informer," Mandel said, talking to the blotter, flipping over a folder. "In fact, I'd say you've done the kid a favor. I'd say—a favor."

Craig's smile fixed on his face as he closed the door, faded as he turned into the parade of citizens hurrying by him to comply with the laws, faded into a thin shadow of doubt.

XII

After two blocks Martin stopped running and leaned against a store front. He must hold on, he said to himself; he must be calm; he must avoid the occasions of panic. Nobody was chasing him really. He glanced back along the sidewalk. A man in a sweater clumsily hauling home the week's groceries. There was no way they could know him, nothing to connect him with the visit to the rectory and the blood on the hearth. He was making it difficult for himself. He must remember that he had his mother's death as an excuse for eccentricity, nothing more. And he mustn't strain that too far. He recalled Mandel's wandering eyes in the theatre lobby; they might light on something sometime, might come abruptly to rest with a stare and a glow of comprehension. He had to be careful.

A woman bundled along the street laboring under two heavy paper bags. He remembered Counihan's around the corner; the grocery store with the card game whiling away on the second floor. He hadn't been there for a long time, two or three weeks. He thought with affection of the soiled cards with bathing beauties on their backs; the waving smoke, the desultory conversation, the jingle of money, and the memory of the peace he had known there, of the belonging, warmed him.

An acknowledged understanding premised the game; each player assumed that the others, like himself, had retreated there to escape a gnawing demand imposed by the routine of the world. They never questioned the right of any other to be present, sedulously avoided any mention of the demand of duty which was held safely at bay by the crooked door and the rubber-padded stairs lest they themselves might be called to account. The dealing and the betting occupied them entirely; the conversation was limited to yesterday's baseball game, exaggerated amatory adventures, dirty jokes, and gossip. It was a haven from the world, a weekly escape from the bills and the nagging; a chance to hold a good hand and to lose measurable stakes; peace carved stubbornly out of the storm of living that raged along the street below the smudged windows.

It was still too early for the funeral home; he might go sit again for a while among the normalcy and the betting, the afternoon simmering softly down while the deck was shuffled and the cards slid over the table.

No one was in sight as he mounted the narrow passageway where the stairs faded up into darkness; the smell of tobacco and the muted voices behind the door associated him with the many Sundays he had come before with the guilt of his mother's worry on his mind and the image of the church dangling tantalizingly before him. At the door, he hesitated: his lips were trembling; his hand sweated on the knob. The old man was not, of course, lurking in the confessional box; the shadows in the church were just shadows. But his brain flagged warnings at him: "Beware" they said; "Watch out." And the film of the murder began to animate itself again; the private showing of the private fear. He was near to tears again. He thrust open the door and went in, dulling his mind with action, sponging out the old images with new ones.

It was like a trip to the past. It could have been any week end of peace; the circle of escape was exactly as he had last seen it. The dealer flipped the cards expertly to each player, the hands moving with mechanical grace, faster than the eye could follow. The players accepted the cards each in his own way; Counihan waited till all five lay overlapped in front of him, then swept them up, aligned them so they looked like one card and spread them stealthily, just enough to reveal one behind the other, stretching out the suspense; O'Doul plucked his off the table one at a time as they slid to a stop before him, like a hen after corn, inspecting the spots eagerly; Shaheen tipped up the corner of each one as it arrived, memorized it sourly and then let it lie disdainfully as he bet; Black huddled his cards close to his chest, applying both hands to them, laying them out atilt on his huge hands. Feet shuffled from time to time under the table; the haze of smoke thickened; a coin rattled onto the table. "Fifty cents," O'Doul said, and pitched accurately so that the half dollar came to rest in the exact center of the circular table. "Huh," said Shaheen.

As Martin closed the door, six pairs of eyes flicked momentarily at him through the smoke; a head turned; a bet was made. Not a beat of the game was lost. It was the custom that no conversation mar the progress of the game. Martin slid into a chair and watched the game move from bet to bet, from mouth to mouth. "Call you," Counihan said and the tension broke. Hands gathered at the pile of coins, the winner laughed, the losers groaned in chorus, a voice resumed a salacious story. Martin breathed easily, felt at home; he looked across at O'Doul, who was stacking his winnings with affection, and grinned.

"Deal you in?" somebody asked him. He nodded, before he remembered the fifty-dollar bill in his pocket, and experienced a moment of doubt, of distrust. What might they say? He had never come before with more than four or five dollars, had never lasted long in the game; usually he dropped out reluctantly before his luck had time to gather steam.

"Some day," a voice said laughingly, "your wife is gonna get wise—" and he was reassured here. The room was like a secret society where none of the proceedings could be breathed outside the charmed circle; the penalty, ostracism. "Deal me in," he said, and put the money on the table, asking for change. "Wow!" a voice said, in mock surprise. "I'll be damned. Lynn must have robbed a bank!" "Look at that!" "Hell's bells, a sharper." But the change was forthcoming, the rumpled bills were counted out limply on the table. The deal began, the conversation was clipped off sharply as though in response to a signal. This was friendship, Martin thought hungrily, scooping up his cards; this was peace.

The ritual ticked away with the afternoon. The money was advanced, the cards circled the table, the stacks fluctuated; the shuffle and riffle and slap of the deck on the wood hushed the room like a gong; the final display of cards lifted the ban and the chatter began again. The old priest plucked at the margin of Martin's mind and was repulsed; the phantoms of detectives faded away before the blankness of the cardboard kings and queens.

Martin began winning. First a pot now and again, then successive victories. Triumph flushed his face; he bet recklessly, laughed raucously, condescendingly patted the losers on their backs. This was living, he thought, stacking the coins carefully, placing his bets with precision, flipping the cards adroitly off the top of the deck—this was part of the new Martin Lynn. He was free now; independence was in him like a fever.

Suddenly he looked up joyously as he gathered in another pot. "You can't beat three aces," he had announced cockily, glorying over the others—and in the gloom beyond the light he beheld Old Man Counihan, who had come up from the store and into the room, noiselessly. Old Man Counihan was staring fixedly at him, silently, with a puzzle in his eyes. Martin dropped his own gaze and concentrated his attention on the game. He wished Old Man

Counihan wouldn't look at him like that; it was threat to his well-being, to his peace. The game began again and the cards sailed in front of him, slipping one underneath the other obediently. Old Man Counihan continued to stare, watching his every move intently as though waiting for a sign of betrayal. What had he heard, Martin thought. What did he know? Why did he have to come up here anyway; it wasn't like him. Especially on Saturday afternoon when he had plenty to do in the store below. Silence suspended the room as the betting began, moving from mouth to mouth like an obscure code, like a ritual. Martin passed when he should have bet; cursed himself as the coins clicked out and the game went on without him. What if Mandel had set spies on him; or the young priest? Maybe they'd found something they hadn't mentioned yet, were waiting for him to betray himself. The game was reduced to O'Doul and Black, who eyed their cards narrowly and bet slowly, cautiously as though escaping detection. The old man's eyes gleamed across the table, the old head motionless in the gloom. Why doesn't he say something, Martin thought; why doesn't he have it out? He could feel the perspiration forming on his forehead; his hands clamming on the pasteboards in his hands; the bathing beauties swam before his eyes.

"I take it!" O'Doul said triumphantly, and the rush of words blotted out his panic; he laughed unnaturally loud at a lewd joke, pounded on the table, announcing noisily that the next one would be his. The deal began and the voices abated. The cards slapped loudly in the silence; the old man was staring again. He's got to go away, Martin thought. They can't follow me around like this. How do you know who to trust? Isn't anywhere safe? And his peace began to crumble, chipping off inside him like stale plaster. And there was a groan and a whir and the performance began all over again in his head. The old priest by the painting, the crucifix, his anger.

He splatted the cards on the table and leapt to his feet. "What are you staring at?" he was screaming, his voice like a silver arrow twanging the air. "Why are you staring at me like that?"

A shocked silence rewarded him; it was as though he had done something indescribably indecent in their view. The hands were paralyzed midway in gathering the cards, in betting; eyes bored at him. Old Man Counihan stretched out a moment to slim eternity and then began to speak.

"You should ask, Martin Lynn," Old Man Counihan said, the lilt of his ancestors lending doom to the voice. "When you're here playing cards with no care in the world and your own mother lying dead at Murray's. Do you call yourself a man, Martin Lynn?"

The voice was like a purr with its odd inflections, its hollow accusation, its controlled, shocked emotion.

"When'd she die?" a voice inquired, tinged with amazement.

"Last night," Old Man Counihan said. "And he her only son and he not paying her the due respect, not according the honor of mourning with her this night. What are you, Martin Lynn?"

The crust of the peace was all gone now, the plaster falling away under the blows of a hammer to reveal rot and ugliness underneath. Martin slumped in his seat, put his arms on the table and buried his head.

"I thought there was something strange about him," O'Doul said, with bitter force. And the chairs scraped back, and the deck fell with a dreadful finality on the table, and feet tramped over the floor. Martin wept without restraint, wept and trembled and gasped noiselessly on the table as the men got up one by one grimly—he could imagine their looks at him—and lifted their coats and hats and straightened their ties and left. No money rattled in the weird stillness; there was only the tramp and shuffle of feet, crossing the floor and clumping heavily down to the street, away from him. The last footfall crept into the distance, the echoes died away, and he heard his own sobbing and it sounded to him like the wailing of the lost souls around the confessional, imploring him. He lifted his head sharply. There was no one left. They had gone as one man, away from his shame, isolating him in the room with his sin, even though they did not know the true extent of it. Even the piles of money remained as they had stood at the end of the last hand; the deck of cards was spread across the expanse of table as the dealer had thrown them. They had not bothered about their winnings. They had sought only to cleanse themselves of him, because he had treated his mother shabbily. If they knew, he thought; if they knew what I've done for her. But they were gone now and he couldn't have told them anyway; could not have rescued his honor by a graver self-accusation.

He sat at the table, staring blindly, numbly as the early evening muffled up the windows, thinking over and over with a kind of detachment: I'm a murderer, a murderer, a murderer. Wherever I go, whatever I do, it will always show, it will always give me away somehow.

There were no conspirators to help him in his search for oblivion; for erasure. He was alone again now. Against the world. There were no allies anywhere. He did not think he could bear the burden any longer, and he sat limply in the gloom waiting for madness to come, staring blankly at the wall and beseeching unconsciousness. But all that came was the old, vivid picture which was a part of him. The priest and the blow and the collapse, over and over again dinning into him. He had no friends at all now except the old priest; they would be inseparable forever.

XIII

Prayer hung in the room like stale air. Steadily since sundown one parish organization after another crowded in to repeat the rosary, huddled solidly from the door to the casket, heel against knee, across the sombre carpet. The Children of Mary, the Sodality of the Blessed Virgin Mary, the Holy Name Society. Rita had forgotten all the old names, the old associations. In breathless falsettos, in uncertain baritones, in strident sopranos, they assailed the Mother of Christ with dissonance. She wished she had never come, had never allowed Mandel to wheedle her, shame her into it. It was as though she were taking all her childhood toys one by one out of an old chest, exposing herself again to enemies she had once conquered, freeing emotions once successfully beaten down. It was like a temptation.

Another group assembled now, composed of both men and women, preparing yet another devotion for her uncle's soul, while he lay white and unheeding against the plush with flowers about his feet. They gathered gradually, the women, in ugly black hats, darting swiftly in and grouping themselves instinctively in twos and threes, bobbing their heads and recalling fresh reasons for lament; the men, stiff and uncomfortable in starch, lumbering hesitantly in, dipping self-consciously at the prie-dieu and backing awkwardly to the farthest possible retreat. Sorrow moaned about the room.

Rita stood by the door, accepting condolences when she was recognized—or when she was pointed out; conscious of the incongruity she represented to their ordered minds. "It's his niece," she had heard a voice croak in the corridor. "Nobody knows where she came from." She later identified the voice with Mrs. Kelley, a scrawny raven of a woman, who had apparently been appointed by the young priest as part of the grim reception committee. But the speaker was inconsequential; the sentiments were general. She was aware of sly glances in her direction, of an intentness in the faces of those who approached her to offer sympathy, and realized with some pleasure that she was adding an additional fillip to their gruesome enjoyment of the occasion, that she shared with her uncle their greedy attention. At least, she exulted defiantly, they recognized that she was not one of them; they knew her superiority. She knew it herself and treasured it as she submitted to the obsequious clutch of their hands, pressing deference at her as she listened to the purr and cackle of their automatic expressions of comfort. She was free of

162

the shackles which bound them in the narrow orbit of their submission. They were robots, duplications ground out by the stultifying process of Mass and sermon and diocesan journal, their thoughts ready-made, their emotions stereotyped, their gestures and voices manufactured. Disgust pecked at her as the same voice went by her again and again, as the same formula of sympathy fell on her ear, as she heard over and over the droning recitation of the Aves. They were all more closely related to her uncle than she was, bound by stupidity; they were his spiritual nieces and nephews and even sons and daughters.

They could have him, she thought; she should never have agreed to come, would not come tomorrow. Certainly she would not attend the funeral.

The group—St. Francis de Sales, she knew now—charity stitched up in a secondhand dress, God worshipped in an old pair of shoes—dropped heavily to its knees and an over-precise, spidery voice took hold of the rosary prayers. She slipped out into the corridor and edged among lingerers and arrivals to a space at the foot of the stairs. She wished that she had arranged with Malcolm to call for her, to rescue her from this. For it was not conceivable that she could bear this another day. She would not, for instance, be able to stave Malcolm away from it and she would not be able to bear his seeing their faces, the stupidity, the clumsiness of these people; her own past vulgarly enacted. She thought it was this she minded most of all; their lack of grace. They wielded their bodies awkwardly like ants with huge burdens; accomplishing the feat but with such struggle as dwarfed the deed itself.

For Malcolm whose contempt for Catholicism, for something she had once laid claim to, was already at an extreme, this vulgar display would be the ultimate straw. And for herself, for her own participation in this childishness, it was a part of her past from which she had shrunk for all her mature years; no need to provide opportunity for it to dig its claws in again. It would have no second chance with her.

She reflected, watching the frumpy clothes, listening to the drone of the prayers, that this sort of thing went on incessantly. The parish activities, the plump women and the thin ones, the bewildered men, the priests like her uncle, maintaining their senseless little islands of superstition amid all the enlightenment; persevering while the world of Malcolm shone and coruscated in their sight, within their reach. The good deeds were imposed, the prayers were mumbled away, the angels sang. She felt—standing in the hall among the devotees—as though she were in prison, trapped in a cell and guarded by uncouth strangers who could not even understand her language.

A murderer among them? It was ridiculous. She had seen among these nonentities, these stuffed beings, no single one that appeared capable of the kind of passion murder required; no capacity for the spectacular sin. Only the minutiae of rebellion: gossip, meat on Friday, white lies, pusillanimous envy—the puny furtive bursts of freedom. Middle class had a meaning in sin, too: the middle range, no grandeur of scale, no courage; the same feints and withdrawals over and over, the repetitious confession month after month; murder required at least a flair, a flourish. She thought perversely: if the murderer is among these people, if he moves and lives and talks and acts and is lost in this labyrinth of the commonplace, he does not deserve even the recognition of arrest. It was after nine o'clock. They would stop coming soon.

The hall had very nearly cleared. Toward the back of the building, Mrs. Kelley croaked at someone over the telephone. She caught snatches: "But I did see him, you know . . . Not well. But I did see him." She seemed to repeat everything as though the world were deaf.

Rita was aware of a boy who stood irresolutely by the door, casting puzzled glances at the slowly-moving figures. He looked at her suspiciously as she advanced toward him.

She smiled wanly, mingling what she hoped was just the right measure of politeness with what she feared was not the right measure of grief.

"In here," she said, with a slight gesture toward the room. "Father Kirkman's in here. They're saying a rosary now." Some urge impelled her to balance her contempt toward them all with a display of kindness to the boy. He was growing into one of them, she thought; the same emptiness of eye, the drawn look around the mouth; his clothing was tight, his hair ragged. She smiled encouragement at him. They are frightened at birth, she thought. But the boy only stared at her, the hunted eyes unwavering, and she became uncomfortable. "Of course, if you'd rather wait—" she said crossly and would have turned from him.

"I—" he began timidly, and she faced him again. He had extended a hand toward her and it remained embarrassedly in the air now. "I'm not looking for Father Kirkman," he said and seemed to speak with difficulty. "I'm looking for my mother."

"Oh, I see," she said, thinking he had come to meet someone. "Perhaps she's inside now. She should be out in a minute." And she saw tears start up in his eyes.

"You don't know," he said, the tightness in his throat screwing up the words. "She's dead. She's here too, dead."

"I'm sorry," she said. "I'll find out." Pity plucked at her as she threaded her way among the women toward the office. It was strange to think of another death somewhere in the building, another body stretched out palely among the flowers, with candles. Strange that she hadn't encountered some sign of it earlier in the evening. She found the mortician, a round, plump man who appeared to be made of rubber, engaged in animated conversation with a younger replica of himself. They were father and son.

"The Lynn boy," the son said, slightly aghast. "We'd better get him upstairs. There's no telling about him."

They swept past her into the hall and she watched them hurrying along toward the boy, the one a slightly defective copy of the other. She followed along the corridor, weaving among the scattered women again, looking curiously at the boy. The father and son stood on each side of him, both whispering to him at once in confidential tones. "Others, you know," she could hear above the drone of the rosary. "Respect . . . careful . . . upstairs." One led and the other followed him up the staircase, contributing gestures and low voices as they went. The boy marched up between them, with his head down, like a prisoner. The father who was last in the entourage, leaned over the railing toward her.

"Thank you, Miss Conroy," he bobbed his head at her.

The boy stopped on the stairs and turned back; placed a hand on the railing and looked at her. His eyes were deeply sad.

"Are you," he began and the words came out in an exhausted flat voice, "are you . . . related to him?" He jerked his head toward the figures in the doorway, toward the hum of the prayer.

"I'm his niece," she said, and wished he had not asked, because she detested the admission; it was like a declaration of loyalty. She saw heads turn away from the rosary to stare at her.

The boy said nothing. But his eyes seemed to grow sadder. He removed his hand from the railing and permitted it to creep up his coat, clutching lightly at his neck. Then he turned and resumed his slow, defeated way up the stairs. Pity stirred in her again. He seemed alone, so poignant, so young. She tried to imagine how it would be to experience a real loss, someone you loved. Her own mother had died long ago, in another world. Was there anyone she could lose that would wreathe her face in such desolation? She tried to imagine Malcolm dead, and could not. But the boy knew what it was like; he bore a burden with him up the carpeted stair.

She steeled herself against the emotion; it didn't do to let pity in, however vagrant and passing. It had claws, too, like her uncle's concern; it dug its way in and refused to budge, snapping at you when you tried to dislodge it. Let the boy mourn; he would recover. Time and the Church would wear him into resignation.

The rosary was finished inside. "May his soul . . ." they

said, and then there was a rustle of movement and a stir of sound that blended into a hum, and they began to crowd out. They spoke to her as they passed. "We're sorry for your trouble," they said. "He was a saint. Nothing less." The vacuous faces filtered past her, nodding and mumbling. A saint! She had never thought of that. In her mind she ranged the fat old priest alongside the lurid asceticism of oleographs, the stiffly-folded hands of the stare-eyed statues. She could find no resemblance. A halo around the gray, wavering head was ridiculous. She took pleasure in remembering what Malcolm had said once: "Saints!" his eyebrows had arched, one corner of his eye pulling up in that faintly cynical characteristic. "I can't imagine anything more disconcerting than somebody always thinking about death. What morbid fellows. Dirty, bearded, going about in hair shirts. I'll bet they never said an amusing word." And the recollection reduced sanctity to a manageable matter, something amenable to whimsy, to Malcolm's sardonic eyebrow. If being a saint meant minding other people's business, certainly her uncle could qualify. If the qualifications included annoyance, meddling, stubbornness, she would concede the title. "St. Francis Kirkman, pray for us," she imagined the extension of the litany, the miracles, the blurred strained pictures in the paper; the fantastic stories which no one ever really believed. She traced with horror her own connection with this imminence; niece to a saint. But Malcolm came to her rescue again, smiling in through the atrocious hats and the awkward, gingerly-smiling men; Malcolm would have made it hilarious somehow.

The mourners filed out, exchanging mutual sorrows, mutual clichés. The dowdy and the cowed, they shuffled out under the green neon light, reluctant, it appeared, to surrender their participation in sorrow, going back to their colorless existences. The yellow shoes and the flowered hats carried on the tradition.

Father Roth came from the back of the building, making his way among the women. They stopped him with questions, expressions of sympathy. "What a blow," Rita heard a plump woman say. "I've been telling them," it was the croaking voice again, "about last night. That sinful man. I saw him going in. As plain as I see you." It was the way the righteous spoke, the girl thought; the voice of insufferable goodness, blaring on like a radio, with all the dripping smugness of the commercial announcer. Some day, she thought with satisfaction, she'll be here too among the flowers and the candles; the tin voice will be silenced as her uncle's was—and perhaps for the same reason.

"It's been good of all of you," the priest was saying. "A work of mercy." Merits were awarded like gold stars in the early grades, the girl thought grimly. "You can go along now."

"We have one more chore," the voice said. The face was obscured from Rita by a wide-brimmed atrocity of flowers. "The Confraternity sent a wreath." They bustled off toward the office. Father Roth saw Rita then and tried to conceal the surprise that showed for a brief moment in his rosy face as he came toward her.

"I didn't know you were coming," he said quietly. Why,

169

there's admiration in his eyes, she thought; he thinks I've come round; that Catholic training is catching up with me after all. "I'm sure it's been an ordeal."

"It's been dreadful," she told him with malice. "These people——"

"It was fine of you to come," he said, and seemed to be apologizing.

"You don't understand," she said harshly, heading off his interpretation of her action as devotion, kindness, love perhaps. But he went on: "You can see how everyone loved him. The devotion he inspired." He gestured vaguely at the fat women and the thin ones, the crestfallen men.

She thought: they do this for every priest, they do this for tyrants, for movie stars. Funerals come cheap. Bernadette, Mussolini, Valentino; it's all the same to them.

"I came because Mandel asked me. He thought I might spot the murderer among the mourners," she said and watched the effect with triumph. Hurt filmed over his eyes, hurt and embarrassment.

"Oh," he said, and the morticians came down the stairs, their eyes cast up in exasperation.

"Father," Albert burst in, "it's that Lynn boy again. Making a fuss about pallbearers. Making another scene."

"Poor boy," the priest said and turned away from Rita, moving off down toward the office with Albert at his heels.

The father beamed at her elbow. "The room's clear now, Miss Conroy," he said, inserting sepulchral tones through the smile. "You can go in—alone. To pay your respects."

He spoke brightly, like a boy who has learned a lesson

170

and is proud. She had been on the point of retrieving her bag and gloves and going out, leaving it behind, saint and all. But the plump, round man who bounced when he walked stood perkily at the doorway, holding the drape aside, inviting her in; providing, she supposed, part of his thoughtful service.

She was not sure she could bear five more minutes of this oppressiveness, five more minutes of morbidity and reminiscence. But from the office the croaky voice battled a buttered one. If she knelt by her uncle a moment, they would perhaps be gone. Five more minutes might be tolerable. She went in.

She crossed the carpet slowly, amazed at the size of the empty room, at the high fragrant banks of flowers, at the still coldness of the old priest who appeared to be stretched comfortably in the coffin, neatly encased in a clean cassock, his hands folded on his breast.

The utter motionlessness of the body appalled her. She found herself expecting that he would move, would extend his hand flatly and emphasize his words with it, as he had used to do, bobbing his head up and down wearily in punctuation. But he remained pale, the lids pasted over the eyes, the skin, in an odd way, encrusted with death. He was gone, she thought, on an excursion into his own theories. She tried to piece out the death according to Catholic doctrine, to apply the generalities to the stubborn old soul which had been her uncle's. By now, by this evening, he had been judged and his deserts accorded him; whether of fire or the Presence; he had made a journey up some slant of misty space and faced his doom. By now, he had seen everything. And the body, laggard that it was, stretched blandly in the coffin, without concern, betraying the soul in its extremity. The hands were folded as primly as though eternity had nothing to do with them.

She dropped to her knees on the prie-dieu and was aware suddenly that the old forces were seizing at her, dragging her back through the years, through the learning, away from the postures she had acquired by such bitter self-denial, back to the narrow beliefs and the childish fears. She had sheared them off so painfully, with such rigorous asceticism of the mind, and they trooped back so eagerly, like children. Constant vigilance was necessary against the traps of childhod, of relaxation, of acceptance. And she looked at the weary, translucent imitation of a man and told herself that this was all, all the delightful sensations of the flesh calmed down to the numbness in the end, to the utter anesthesia of death. He had seen everything and knew, of course, by now that there was nothing.

A faint, barely audible cry escaped behind her. Like an animal's. She turned and saw the boy. He stood just inside the door, staring at the corpse, and he was swaying from side to side as though the sight of death drained all his strength.

XIV

Martin had come through the streets toward the funeral home in a haze of numbness; it was as though snow blanketed the earth and muffled up all the sounds and dimmed the perspective; nothing seemed to touch him, to come near him, to recognize him. Pedestrians blurred as they loomed up before him and faded away to the side; he moved along as a ship cuts water splitting the flood to each side. Automobiles cleared his path, dogs wagged warily away from him. It must show, he thought; like a disease; his guilt must stand out on him like a rash, visible to everyone.

They moved away from me, too, he thought remembering the chairs scraping back at Counihan's, the distaste as the cards slipped onto the table. He carried somewhere underneath his clothes a bell, like a leper. They had shunned him; the charmed circle had looped away, abandoning him outside. And they didn't even know, he thought; they didn't know the half of it. They thought he was besmirching his mother's memory; they didn't know to what lengths he had gone to protect it, to exalt it even.

What if, he thought with panic, the promised land of freedom did not contain all the sweets he had anticipated? What if, in asserting himself, in throwing off the chains, he had disposed as well of comradeship, of geniality, of love? He envisioned an eternity of emptiness, of men avoiding him, of detours around his independence. But it wouldn't be that way, it couldn't be. And he told himself again that any existence was an improvement over the indigence he had known before, the poverty of pocket and of heart. Laboriously, as a man shifts a burden, he focused his attention to other things.

He tried to remember, for instance, if he had retrieved his money from the abandoned stacks of silver on the card table. But distraction blurred the details. He thought suddenly of the confessional and the old priest waiting in the dark, cocking an ear toward his repentance.

And he seemed to be whirling round and round in the huge room with the blank walls, surrounded by priests sitting smugly behind grills; only they were not always the old priest; sometimes the lean, preoccupied face of the detective, Mandel. They were all waiting for him to speak. But there was no sound anywhere. The confessional boxes floated round and round him on a sort of carousel and he was first in line; behind him the poker players shifted impatiently, casting disapproving glances in his direction. But he could not go in; he could not move. "I did it for my mother," he told them over and over. But they only scowled. And then a green light blotted out all of them and the green light said: "J. T. Murray & Son, Thoughtful Service," and he went up the steps and stood in the corridor in bewilderment. He was vaguely aware of the girl talking to him, saying something about the old priest. And he thought how beautiful she was—like the slick, smoothly-contoured girls in the advertisements, the luscious desires that languished on the billboards, and then he was going up the stairs and she said, "I'm his niece."

The words swept through him like a cold wind. She shared his sorrow, he thought, staring blankly at the symmetrical, polished face; she knew what it was like to have the familiar niche suddenly empty, to have the furniture of the world rearrange itself grotesquely with the most important piece left out. He thought he would like to sit somewhere cool and quiet and talk to her about it. And he reddened, wondering if she saw the sin in him, if his degradation were visible to her deep eyes; and when it struck him like a light flashing suddenly on that he was

174

the cause of her sorrow, he turned and fled up the stairs behind Albert. And the thought sickened him like a blow in the stomach; and the whirl in his head began again, all the incomprehensible facts racing round at the rim of his brain; the death of his mother, the priest falling down, the detectives popping up, the confessional like a threat in the shadows. They circled and circled as he clumped up the stairs behind Albert—so fast that the total effect in him was rest, inertia, as a wheel turns until the spokes are invisible, and the hub still. He must think, he told himself, he must think. The thoughts must remain quiet for a moment so he could look at them, examine them sanely. Other events waited outside the circle, alternatives, denials, affirmations; other endurances were to be borne before the end.

Albert stepped aside and he saw high candles glimmering over a vaguely familiar face; a thin, peaceful face with almost no hollows for the shadows to rest in. He tried to remember under what conditions he had seen the face; its associations were those of stress, of worry, of shame, and yet of love. But as he moved toward it and the strange kind of bed on which it lay—a box with a lined lid—he told himself he was mistaken; it was only that it resembled somebody he had once known, back before the horror began. Then he saw the dress in which the body was clothed, neatly and with an absurd dignity, and he knew it was his mother's face which had been somehow contorted into peace.

It was like the fulfillment of a wish; she looked as he had always wanted her to look: serene, even radiant; mirth beamed in the lines around the mouth which worry had dug; she looked happy at last. Refreshment and light, he thought; peace. "It's all right," he said aloud, and Albert coughed warningly behind him and he didn't care. She was safe; out where they couldn't touch her, couldn't strike at her. He realized with a rush that there had been no use in murder after all; she would have smiled thus under any ministrations. It was death and not death's minions that composed the face, no matter what deathly juices Albert had inserted in her veins. She was beyond his pity now, beyond his futile lunges at revenge in her behalf. He found himself envying her; she was out of it all and he was left behind among the enemy, abandoned like a baby on the cold doorstep of the world; she had betrayed him into trouble beyond her worst fears. She didn't know what worry was, he thought; she had the luck after all. His last ally was gone. He was alone against them all now. Nobody would soothe his poor sin now.

"One detail, Mr. Lynn," a voice said and he was galvanized into a feeble hate as he recognized Albert's polite whine. "One small thing." Albert's face looked yellow in the candlelight. "About pallbearers. If you wish, we shall be happy to provide them—for Monday morning. It will save you the trouble of summoning—friends." Albert's large eyes roamed the room, seemed to accentuate its emptiness. "If you want to leave it in our hands——"

Pride pricked at Martin, stirring him out of his lethargy of guilt and pity, urging him on again. "You mean, hire them?" he said hollowly, his anger exaggerating the volume of his voice.

"It is a common practice," Albert said, his professional glibness mechanizing the words. "We keep men available for just such occasions. Dignified, appropriate-looking men. Like friends of the family."

"Listen here," Martin shouted at him, his voice trembling the candles. "You needn't think we haven't got enough friends." He could hear the chairs scraping back, the cards dropped on the table. "We have plenty of friends." He thought, this is a lie; it doesn't matter now but it's a lie. "If you hadn't hidden her away up here on the second floor while that priest downstairs——"

"Please," Albert hushed him with flat, nervous hands. "Please. They're praying downstairs."

"They better pray," Martin said. "He needs it. Now you get out of here and don't come bothering me about pall-bearers."

"All right, all right," Albert said, pressing the words out precisely and angrily as though with a die. "I just wanted to help."

"Help." Martin snarled at him as the dapper figure flashed through the door. He thought this was a man worth killing; this was a man who might die beneficially. The habit of the upraised hands coursed through his muscles. He remembered the body then, and that he was alone with it and the echo of his own voice and the splutter of the candles which was like a low whisper in the room. He knelt by the bier.

"I didn't mean it, Mother," he looked earnestly into the calm face, thinking that she must have overheard his thought of death. "I didn't mean any of it. You know I'm a good boy." The still, strange lips had spoken the phrase to him many times in approval and promise. "I just wanted everything to be—nice," he told the dead body. "I

177

wanted a nice funeral." He beseeched an answer from her, his eyes yearning toward the closed lids, seeking a testimonial which would endorse his actions. But nothing came.

Briefly, he had the impression she was breathing and he fixed his eyes on the black-clothed outline to catch the familiar rise and fall which differentiated life from death. He would have touched her but that the memory of the chill was still on him from the night before. The body was motionless; only his own breath coughed raspily at him. Whatever he had done, whatever he was, she could not help him now. She had escaped, sliding quickly down the wall in the basket like St. Paul. She was out of it; she was free; he was the one enslaved.

"I thought it would help," he told her desperately, thinking of the crucifix flashing through the air. "You see how I felt, don't you?" Regret knelt with him by the corpse; regret and futility. He had committed sin and had no one to share it with, hysterically acting out some ridiculous comedy which was forever private. He had plunged into disaster for nothing, had set up an unnecessary round of crime and shame which would ring him in the end.

"I'll give myself up," he told her listlessly, and thought of the shocked expressions, the dismay, the priest praying at him. He thought of handcuffs and that they might be cool, and of bare brick walls and iron bars. The confessional was closed to him; he had beaten it off, but the police would serve; any mother would do now, any forgiveness. "It was a mistake," he said and remembered how glibly he had pronounced the small, pink sins through the grill; impure thoughts, anger, cursing; he had moved now into a region where the actions were not translatable into ambiguous euphemisms—pride, murder, hating the Church, whatever it was.

"I'll go down and tell them," he said. "Maybe they'll give me pallbearers from the prison. Fellow convicts." He smiled crookedly at her, imagining a cell block lined with peering, haunted faces—brothers who would look at him and understand. "I'll give myself up. It'll be a relief." He had a sensation as of silence after a deafening noise; as of wind cleaving freshly into heat. "May her soul and all the souls of the faithful departed," he mumbled audibly, "rest in peace." He moved down the stairs, thinking with something like anticipation that he had never seen the interior of a jail; that it was curious that the confessional box had a grill set into it like the square in a dungeon door. He wondered vaguely if the police would permit him to attend the funeral.

XV

Father Roth came from confessions to the funeral home at ten o'clock, oppressed by a disquieting thought. Earlier in the evening, as he donned his stole and took his place between the converging ranks of penitents, it occurred to him that he might hear whispered to him out of the darkness the self-accusation of murder; that the voice which had been the last one Father Kirkman had heard might reappear in the shadows. "I confess to Almighty God and to you, Father, that I have killed a man." The thought was like cold air across his shoulders; the murderer inches away from him, breathing out the personal offense, entreating mercy. Suppose he should hear it, hear it recounting the circumstances unmistakably, hear it repent—and then hear it rebel against the legal, secular surrender to the police? The hackneyed dilemma was taken suddenly from the text books and deposited heavily in his lap; the seal of confession in practice and not theory. And he prayed for grace and listened—but it did not happen, after all. The pattern of impiety was as usual; murder did not intrude.

But the possibility remained with him as he let himself into the back door of Murray's—into the efficient office where the corpses and the mourners were tabulated neatly by the slovenly girl—the possibility that the culprit might be one of his own flock, might sit dutifully in the pews tomorrow morning, compelled by habit to observe the weekly devotion.

The multiple voice of prayers muttered along the corridor toward him; heads nodded in deference and sympathy. If it were someone he knew—however slightly—would he be able to walk resolutely up to Mandel and turn him over? Sacrifice the solicitude of the shepherd to the demand of the hireling? Was there not a question of duty beyond the strict statutes of the legal process? His memory of procedure was clear; he must plead with the penitent to confess, to accept humbly the legal and material consequences of his sin. His personal allegiance was plain as well; Father Kirkman had been his superior, his advisor, his friend; the apprehension of his killer would be balm to his own anger, his own loyalty. But beyond the definite boundaries of orthodoxy loomed the horizon of the soul in distress, the frail fluttering of the wings, wounded and pierced by sin, flailing pitiably to earth. "Let it not be one of these," he prayed to himself, his eyes going round the commonplace faces in the office: Mrs. Kelley, Mrs. Garagiola, Mrs. Brown, Tom Linthicum . . . "Let it be someone I do not know, or let me not find it out first." He was ashamed of his timidity in the face of danger. If the choice came, he knew he would have to make it; who was more his brother's keeper?

"What a nice young priest this morning," a placid, motherly face fished up irrelevancies to lighten the atmosphere.

"Father Lewis," he said, smiling his faint, automatic smile. Details brushed away his torture; had he been clear about what Masses the substitute was to say on the following Sunday morning?

"So peaceful," the voice went on, glancing toward the mumble of prayer. "Such a lovely appearance." His own mind followed the switch of thought to Father Kirkman tardily. Perhaps he had better call Lewis and make sure. He made his way toward the telephone. Joseph Timothy Murray harangued him briefly about arrangements for Monday and Mrs. Kelley complained whiningly that there wasn't room for all the flowers and what should she do? before he finally sat down at the desk and pulled the instrument toward him. He searched his pockets for the notation he had made of the phone number the chancery had given him and spread the small square of paper before him on the polished surface. He flattened it with one hand and dialed with the other, while the voices buzzed around him in the small room and the death in the front parlor pervaded the conversation. His day had included a

visit to the Archbishop and he had stood awkwardly before the worried-looking prelate and explained about
Father Kirkman in an improbable voice. "A valuable serv-
ant," the Archbishop had said, and later, "We know not
the day nor the hour," in a tired, strained voice, applying
death to himself, Father Roth guessed, testing his dim
eyes down the paths of eternity. If the Archbishop heard
murder in the confessional tonight, would he be complicated and confused by the bleating sheep, the wandering
soul?

The dial mechanism clicked and the muted ringing began. His eyes rested absently on the square of paper on
which he had preserved the name and the phone number.
He remembered scrawling awkwardly on the pad while
his eyes looked over the edge of the desk at the dead body;
he had written mechanically, heard mechanically. He
looked again at the paper now and thought Father Kirkman may have rested his hand on this while the hand was
still warm.

The electric light overhead glazed on the paper as he
stared. He was aware of markings on it that he had not
noticed before; not writing, but faint impressions rutted
into the paper just below his own notations: a series of
vertical marks intersected here and there by curves. He
inspected it more closely, finding that he must keep his
eyes at a certain angle to prevent the glare obscuring the
marks. They were the echo of writing, dug into the sheet
by the weight of a pencil that had written on the pad-
sheet above it, the kind of copy without carbon that results dimly on one sheet of paper beneath another. He remembered that Mandel had inspected the pad closely for

evidence and found nothing—not writing at any rate. Had a page been torn off? And by the murderer? He craned his neck, seeking the exact angle, a clear revelation of the slight engraving in the pulp. Only some of the letters were visible. The ringing in the telephone ceased and a voice spoke metallically. He made out an M in the reflected writing and then another letter and gradually the entire thread was legible to him. "Hello, hello," the voice in his ear was annoyed now, but he stared silently at the white paper with the shadow of a name on it. Finally he answered. "Hello," he said and thought his own voice sounded even farther off than the voice on the instrument. It couldn't be—he tried to concentrate on the scratchy tones coming down the wire—it couldn't be that Martin Lynn had done it, even if his name is imprinted here in Father Kirkman's handwriting.

XVI

At the foot of the stairs, in the deserted hall, Martin met Mrs. Lally. "I forgot my prayerbook," she said, wheezing, opening her mouth to reveal the spaces between the scarce teeth. "I was with her all evening. Doesn't she look lovely now?" Her aged skin had the appearance of being perpetually soiled; in places the lines were so thick they imparted an effect of pencilings. He was back for a moment in the miserable apartment house, fighting his way against all the old resourceful enemies. His confession would lift him onto a plane of violence away from her and her kind, anyway. The fat undertaker labored down the hall, extinguishing lights as he went.

"We could go along together," Mrs. Lally was saying, "after I get the book. It's a time for company."

Wherever I go, Martin thought, it will not be back to the old life, to people like this; conviction and jail will at least break that monotony. The mourners seemed to have gone now; there was no sound and little light from the parlor where the priest lay. Through the draperies he could see a solid shaft of flowers.

"I'm going to stop in here for a prayer," he mumbled at her and crossed the corridor, hearing her cluck her tongue softly against her few teeth; she was pitying him, he knew. She had no idea of what he was capable of—what he had done—he thought grimly, and went through the curtains and into the pallid, muffled atmosphere of death. A girl knelt with her back to him; but he barely saw her. In the gloom the old priest's prettified face glowed at him and he cried out before he could control himself. For there was peace here too on the stretched and grayish skin, like lacquer sprayed over the cold face, and though it had the appearance of being applied from the outside, he felt it might belong there.

The girl turned to look at him; he had an impression of high forehead, luminous eyes, a pale smooth face which mirrored bewilderment. "I'm sorry," he told her. "I'm sorry I yelled."

"It's nothing," she said in a flat voice, and turned away from him, back to the stony face with the unearthly calm on it. It was the niece, he remembered, and traced in the back of her head the poise and slickness. She gave little evidence of grief, he thought—but that was what class did for you.

184

"Did you love him?" he asked, with unaccustomed bold-ness and tried to decide if he should confess to her.

"Love him?" She repeated it dully, as though she did not understand the words. She seemed to be looking again at the corpse, to make sure what this thing was that might be an object of devotion. He wondered if she were married to a confident young Catholic of the kind who passed the collection baskets on Sunday and had attended a school famed for football.

"I don't know," she said. And after a while: "No. I didn't love him."

Martin was shocked. "He was your uncle," he said in-credulously. The sign of any deviation toward sin that was not his own surprised him; he had forgotten the numerous brotherhood he had joined.

"Maybe I did. Maybe I did. I don't know," she said in a singsong desperate voice and he looked at her quickly, ex-pecting to see her head going from side to side in despair, like an old woman keening, but she had not moved. "Somebody killed him." She said it as though she were trying to convince herself of an incredible thing. "Can you understand how somebody killed him?"

"Yes," he said at once, and felt warm among the candles and the flowers and the girl's voice. It was like an intima-tion of the world he had despaired of; a world where people like this girl talked casually of sin, beyond Mrs. Lally and the priest, beyond his mother even: the rarefied atmosphere above poverty and denial. He could talk to her about it; she'd understand how it was. There were better visions than the cell blocks and the row of criminal faces; there were other allies, after all.

"How could they?" the girl asked. "Whatever they wanted, how could they kill him. He was old and weak."

"He was strong," the boy said, fixing his eyes on the face that had been splotchy in life. "He was power. And stupidity. Superstition. The Church. You don't know how strong he was."

She moved her head suddenly so that he looked at her. He thought of telling her how anger coiled around you, wrapping you for years, teasing you with strength until it finally squeezed, promising you glory and greatness and freedom.

"But who?" she said. "I can understand thinking about it, planning it even—but doing it. . . ."

"There are lots of reasons," he said. "For love even." The word rubbed on his lip. "Maybe they didn't mean to do it at all, though. Maybe they were—thought they were—killing the Church. It just happened to be him—to be your uncle." The "they" kept it impersonal, objective. He didn't have to give himself up—not yet. "They just grabbed something and it was all over maybe. Never thinking."

Martin watched the square, tailored shoulders, the hair pushing out along the rim of the hat. "Somebody—not right," she said. "Somebody psychotic. Not responsible."

"Not responsible," he said happily, repeating it like a lesson. "That's it. Not responsible." The idea was like a door opening in the blank room, letting in a breath of freedom. The scent of the flowers around the casket was heavy in his nostrils, blotting out the stench of death. He breathed it in gratefully, along with the exonerating idea,

186

took refuge in the pretense. "You understand." He looked fondly at her.

Her reply was barely audible; she did not look at him. "I understand," she said and the silence stretched like a bond between them. I'm not licked yet, he thought; after all, I didn't really promise anybody. His mother would not rise up to hold him to anything now. He remembered Mandel with his soft, wandering eyes, and the young priest, and the two detectives in the diner, the prison bars and the confessional. They didn't have him yet.

A scratchy voice cut across the comfort from outside the draperies, advancing along the corridor. "I did see him," it said. "Just as plain as I see you. I saw him go right into the rectory just as bold as you please."

"Why didn't they pick her?" the girl said suddenly, turning to him, her face furry against the candles. "Why didn't they kill somebody useless like her—" She jerked a gesture toward the corpse, "—instead of him." It was as though the sight of death had finally stirred grief in her.

The voice sawed on outside. "He rang the bell and looked in the window and went in. Oh, I'd recognize him again, let me tell you."

"Who's that?" the boy breathed sharply in the room. "Who's that talking?" The voice rattled on, repeating its authority proudly.

"Some woman," the girl said in disgust. "She saw him. She saw who did it. She knows. But she didn't stop them."

Now she'll have to be stopped, he thought; that voice didn't understand; it would have to be cut off. The door slammed and the voice halted abruptly, resumed in a distant murmur, fading away.

"She's got to shut up," the boy said with a kind of deliberate indignation, and got to his feet. "She doesn't know how it is." He moved abreast of the girl, stood looking down at her, rubbing his hands awkwardly against the sides of his trousers. They were conspirators speaking in a code. "Not like you," he smiled, then glanced darkly at the door. "She's got to shut up." He walked resolutely to the door. The scratchy voice couldn't be far away; he could take no chances. Deliverance still awaited him somewhere; there was a level of light and refreshment some place, peopled by the girl's equals. "Flaming Love" the movie poster had said. "Breath-taking thrills." It was a matter of going the whole way, of blotting out the commandments, the denials, the threats—the blurred confessional boxes in the blank-walled room—and going on, past feeling, past responsibility, past the repetitious tableau in the brain.

Outside the neon light had been switched off; in the darkness under the marquee he could hear a chatter of voices along the quiet street. He began to follow, wondering what would be in reach of his anger this time. He hoped it would not be another crucifix.

XVII

Rita gasped as he left and knelt coldly in the gloom as the front door closed behind him. She heard his footsteps slipping down the stones in the stillness and tried to remember what she had said to him in the whispers they had unconsciously assumed. She had the impression he was acting somehow on her suggestion, going out because she had sent him, on an errand of her devising. "Not responsible." She remembered his voice, his face. They had talked with a peculiar, frightening intimacy. She wanted suddenly to call him back, to tell him she had not meant anything—whatever it was. He seemed destined to act on all her impulses, to put into action all her tentative supposings. He was following the woman with the grating voice; he was following the woman home. Because—because he feared what the woman had seen? Because he had killed her uncle?

She got to her feet and came quickly out into the hall. At the doorway she stopped. The young priest stood there, leaning against the newel post at the foot of the stairs, staring blankly at the front door. Behind him, Mandel came slowly, casually along the corridor from the rear; he was like a man out for a stroll. He stopped and stood between them.

"Well?" he said. But neither of them spoke. She could hear the candles fluttering in the room behind her, could smell the flowers.

If the boy were the murderer. . . . And they had spoken so familiarly in the calmness beside the corpse, meeting in a strange common ground of her desires and his actions. Why, I agreed with him, she thought; I approved. "You understand," he had said; she remembered the look he had given her, as though they shared a secret. Perhaps, she thought, they did.

Mandel waited expectantly, looking for a report from his spy. He had counted on the tie of blood, on some hidden subsurface devotion beating beneath the skin that death would pick out with a cold thumb to identify her with her uncle. But there were relationships closer than joint ancestry; the dim, revolting kindred of sin, lashing stranger to stranger, a secret society where the countersign was exchanged by eyes, by atmosphere. If she told Mandel about the boy, she should certainly tell the priest about herself; her wish had fathered his thought; he had committed the sin which only cowardice had denied her.

And where was he now, with his frightened eyes and grim, trembling voice? Where were they both now? How close were they to the old woman, who perhaps did deserve to die?

Mandel said "Well?" again, but still neither of them replied.

XVIII

Martin could see three figures plodding along under the street lights, moving slowly, as though without purpose, moving out of the glow into the darkness and on into the next glow. Now and then he could hear the rattle of their voices against the houses, the hedges, the curbstone trees; the scratchy voice was loudest. They foresaw no doom; for them an ordinary Saturday night drew to a close a quite ordinary week. At an intersection, they paused carefully for the traffic and he paused with them, half a block behind in the night. So cautious about the cars, he thought, and would have smiled if he had not been so tense.

A block later, one of them went off up a side street, waving gaily in the darkness and the two went on together, talking in subdued voices. Martin followed, maintaining a discreet distance, his eyes intent on them, walking softly over the stones, tensing as he crackled leaves under his feet.

It was like gripping the crucifix; impressions twisted and whirled in his head, fingers inside his face seemed to be pressing against his eyeballs, hands plucked and looted among his entrails, but he walked down the street after the women. He felt as though he were rounded in by a dark tunnel where a single light was visible at the end toward which he labored; he was aware of objects and persons around him but they were obscured and gloomed by the blackness and the light alone had purpose and incentive. Like a mechanical thing he had been pointed toward an objective and he arrowed unerringly to it, oblivious of obstructions. There was only one way open to him without disavowal, and he took it, slipping over the pavement in the dark, working from one pool of light to the next, with the confusion flapping inside him and the horror writhing in his head, going along after the tin voice that threatened to expose him. Like a distraction—like a barely distinguishable sideway off the tunnel, he remembered his decision to surrender himself to the police; but the light at the end of the cone was brighter, drawing him on. He knew that his mother and the old priest were lying dead somewhere but the memory of them was like that of the elusive name that suggests itself enticingly at the corner of the mind and bobs out of reach before it can be fully recalled. Everything except the scratchy voice which bobbled back toward him on the wind was a half-reality only. The tunnel pulled him on.

It was vaguely like the huge blank room where he had thrown himself frenetically against the high solid walls; he had a feeling that if all the lights were turned on, he would see the confessionals again. But reflection was denied him. He stumbled on over the lines of the paving stones, trying to remember stealth.

At a street corner, he was afraid he had lost the two women and quickened his pace until he could make them out murkily in the shadows ahead of him. It seemed a darker street than the others and he peered intently ahead; he pressed his eyes against the gloom stretching away beyond him and knew of a sudden where he was. It was the street in which the church stood—the church and the rectory. The woman, of course, lived opposite them; there she had sat, at one of these windows, and watched him go up the rectory steps; she would know him again. He clenched his teeth and stared at the dim shapes ahead of him. But there seemed to be only one now. If he had lost her. . . .

"Goodnight," the tin voice said and a white hand blurred in the light from the street lamp. He breathed easier; it was the other one that had gone, departing into one of the doorways that intervened between himself and his quarry. The figure that had spoken diminished down the block. They must be near her home now.

"Hey," he shouted abruptly, the sound shattering down among the high, old-fashioned housefronts. The figure stopped, turned. The innocence, he thought—and shouted again. "Wait a minute." It wouldn't do to let her get inside the house; no telling what the situation was there: husband, children, even at this hour. This was the place, here where the street was deserted and they were alone in the friendly gloom. The voice scratched something at him among the trees and he broke into a trot, going along toward her.

He was aware that across the street in the formless hulk of the church building the confessional boxes lurked, shrouded now in blackness, waiting for him; and within sight of this spot the old priest had been struck down without warning. His sins were localized on the map; huddled together narrowly; one X might cover them all.

"Did you call?" the voice rasped at him like chalk on a slate, and even her affability was grotesque. She held an enormous black handbag before her like a shield; her hat bobbed; he could see that she had a long, thin neck and protruding teeth. Going around talking, he thought bitterly; minding everybody's business. She was the other side of the coin, the priest's counterpart and creation; the obeyer, totting up carefully the merits she accrued in heaven; daily Communion, first Friday, novena, benediction. She standardized goodness, reducing it to mass production and mediocrity.

"I did," he said and his voice trembled between them. They were barely two yards apart. His hands fumbled at the sides of his trousers and the long neck tempted him.

"Yes," he said. "Yes, I called." It's sin, he thought clearly. The light glimmered dangerously near; the end of the tunnel approached. A street lamp shadowed the branches of a tree in weird designs on her face. She seemed to be squinting at him, tilting her head back slightly, elongating her throat. A gold tooth gleamed at him. It's sin, he thought, but it doesn't matter now; already he was beyond the pale; he had twined his fingers across the body of Christ; he was past redemption anyway.

"What is it, young man?" She was not annoyed; her mouth twisted into a grotesque smile. She was being kind; forcing the virtue into the face of danger. She didn't know, either; no disturbing particles pumped through her thin, prim blood; she'll be better off dead, he thought; maybe the truth will dazzle her. Voices skirled in his head: the old priest was leaning out of the confessional now, beckoning; he was angry, tired of waiting. Martin stepped forward out of the shadows, his elbows at his waist, his hands extended forward as though to receive alms. I'm gone forever now, the message flashed in his mind; nobody will ever say no to me again. He would, he knew, feel the bones and the cartilage writhing in his hands.

But headlights beamed among the trees, tires squealed behind him, a door clicked open and a voice came across the darkness like a hand. "May I give you a lift?" It was cheerful and polite. He spun toward it, and knew even before the head in the aperture was clear to him, that it was the girl; her silhouette echoed the one he had looked at fondly in Murray's parlor. Perfume drifted toward him. She was in a cab, leaning forward from the back seat. He looked from her to the woman who stood in perplexity now on the pavement in the spotty light.

"Thanks," he said, and the word was like a groan.

"Well, I must say—" the woman chattered to herself. "You never know. Stopping me like that——"

He got into the cab and pulled the door shut, closing off her words. He sat forward on the seat in the darkness as the motor ground into higher gear, not daring to look toward her shadow in the dark. He found himself trembling and perspiring.

"I just happened to see you," she said shakily, and he was convinced of her nervousness, her own relief. How much had she seen? "Where do you live?"

Where indeed? he thought: in the second floor parlor at Murray's; in the confessional box. He mumbled the old address at the driver. He looked toward her but her scent, rich and pungent, was clearer than his sight of her. "Did you follow me?" he asked her, breathing heavily, and clapped one hand upon another in the gloom to still their rattling. The driver, his own huge hands showing on the wheel in the dashlight, began to whistle.

"You stopped me," he said when she didn't answer, and the car rumbled and whirred and the whistle continued.

"Stopped you?" she said, but the surprise was not genuine. She wants me to say it, he told himself bitterly; she wants me to confess; but the admission was like a bone in his throat; he had to speak around it. "We're both mourners," she said moodily.

"I would have been glad if I'd done it. I wish you hadn't come along." He was like a child deprived of a treasure.

"Done what?" she insisted.

"You know," he said, and lurched as the cab turned into his street. There was a movement from her and he was aware of emotion radiating from the darkness around her. "You've got to stop it." She was almost pleading. "You can't go on. It's— It's—" She could get no further. She seemed to shrink into herself, into her shell of control, of propriety.

"How can I stop?" He was taunting her now. "You said I wasn't responsible." But there was no answer. "We're not enemies," he tried to tell her wearily, his own voice pleading now. "We understand. All the superstition, the people hemming you in. The woman, the priest. You hated him, too."

The whistling and the cab stopped together. The driver reached a long arm across and pressed the catch, swinging the door open.

"Goodnight," Martin said and probed the gloom trying to see her. He thought suddenly: a good-looking girl is bringing me home in a cab. But the thought continued logically, relentlessly: she has just prevented a murder, hindered me from sin. It was not how he had ever imagined it. He was conscious down somewhere beneath the fear and the sin and the agitation, of a vague square window, but she was only a shape in the darkness and she did not speak. The cab drew noisily away from the curb and he stood lonesomely in the night, watching the red tail-light diminish in the distance.

There was elation in him, even among the agonies. That was the world to which he might attain; the smooth, untroubled world where sin had no foothold as a menace; brilliant and comfortable and friendly. And he thought with scorn of the psychiatrist who had shaken his head and shown pity. He would come into his own, yet.

Still she had followed him to prevent another killing. All his memories returned with a rush; the old priest, the crucifix, his mother and the detective. The girl would tell them; he had revealed himself, if not in so many words, still unmistakably. She would repeat her suspicions and they would come for him. Relief tinged him again with a faint glow; the confessional presented itself again and a hand beckoned from the curtains and then a face appeared, but it was not Father Kirkman—it was Mandel, the detective. He remembered again the grill and the bars. They'll come and get me, he thought, and believed he would be glad. It would be order again; arrangement among the conflicting images. It would be peace. The girl might be doing him still another favor.

But in the hallway the two detectives were waiting and when they came toward him, he was conscious only of terror, bubbling away in his loins, weakening him.

XIX

After the girl had gone out the front door, the young priest and the detective stood silently at the foot of the stairs. Albert's high, intense voice sounded from the office behind them. Slow, heavy feet plodded overhead.

"She wasn't much help," Mandel said finally, looking after the girl thoughtfully. "Not even a report. That's the trouble with amateur assistants. No sense of proportion. No feeling for the small indication. Just because the murderer didn't come in and confess—" He shrugged. "Still I guess there wasn't anything for her to see."

They heard a movement up the stairs and looked up at Mrs. Lally, who was padding painfully down, clinging to the banister with the desperation of the old. "Martin," she said. "Martin," before the old eyes recognized the priest. "It's you, Father Roth," she said. He smiled up at her, forcing politeness through his confusion. "Two at once," Mrs. Lally, laboring down the stairs, said sadly. "We used to say they always died in threes." Would she know? the priest asked himself. Would she have any idea what lay behind the faint impressions of a name on a sheet of paper? He looked at Mandel. The detective had turned away toward the room where the priest lay and was now moving through the doorway; he had had enough of gabbling women.

"Mrs. Lally," the priest said. "Did you see Martin Lynn the night his mother died?" He glanced nervously toward the parlor door, feeling like a criminal himself.

"Oh, yes." She spoke in a loud, hollow sibilance. "Poor lad. I saw him just before I called you, Father. He was out of his head with grief. His mother was all he had." Tears spotted the old eyes. "I don't know what he'll do now."

"Why didn't he wait for me to come?" the priest asked, thinking that Mandel must be able to hear and hoping these would sound like normal questions for a priest to be asking a parishioner. Sooner or later, he would have to tell the detective about the piece of paper, whether he had discovered the motive behind the sin or not.

"He didn't know what he was doing." Mrs. Lally flavored everything with her pity. "He went out—till all hours. Walking the streets. Came back limp as a rag. As though he'd been crying. Poor boy."

It was not, of course, proof. Martin's name might have been there for any number of reasons, all innocent. There was no definite link.

"Maybe it'll bring him back to the Sacraments," Mrs. Lally said, sniffling slightly. "He hasn't been since his father died." The priest remembered Martin's words as he came to in the office at Murray's. "You wouldn't fix anything, you priests—" He recalled the haggard face coming up the stairway from the basement, the fear in the eyes. The spurning of grace laid the soul open to unexpected dangers.

"We could take the lady home," Mandel was saying from the doorway. "It's late. I got the car out there."

If the boy did it, the priest thought—if Martin Lynn had actually killed Father Kirkman, his duty lay before him. But he came back always to the torture of the young face, the suffering, the signs of . . . remorse? Martin was his strayed lamb, in any case; if he delivered the boy up to the wolves of the law, to a cold-hearted justice which was not at all concerned with forgiveness, the sin might be confirmed and imbedded. If he granted Martin some time—no matter how brief—of freedom, the dark convolution of motive which lay behind the act might straighten itself into repentance.

Mandel had opened the door and offered his arm to Mrs. Lally. He was assisting her down the steps now, supporting her delicately with a hand under her arm. He did not look like a wolf of the law, certainly; more like a sheep dog, the shepherd's friend.

There were other, grimmer possibilities. The boy might not be sane, on one hand; on the other, he might take the margin of time at its biggest advantage and make his escape. They were chances he must take, paying out the strand of hope in the anticipation of some larger benefit, in the gamble for the repentant soul, the sheep crouched pitiably on the grass, bleating to be found.

He went down the steps behind the halting woman and the detective, praying that the thin thread of his trust would endure.

XX

When Mandel got back to headquarters, they had brought Craig in. He was limp, disheveled, unsmiling. "I thought we'd finished the inquisition," he said sullenly.

"Something turned up. You don't look like yourself."

Craig lit a cigarette shakily. His coat was stained, his tie-knot had slipped away from his collar, his hair straggled.

"Where'd they find you?" Mandel inquired innocently. "Looks like it was quite a place."

"A place," Craig said, "I'm going back to as soon as this comedy is over. I told you I was nowhere near that movie theatre. If you're going to get so particular, I'll produce witnesses."

"Blondes, I'll bet," Mandel was reminiscent. "It was always blondes. Loyal, trustworthy maidens."

Craig looked up darkly. Then he relaxed his face, stretched languidly in the chair, retreating behind his usual nonchalance. Mandel wondered what the army had done with Craig. "This time, strangely enough," Craig drawled dreamily, "it would be a brunette. It would be worthwhile for you to get her down here just for a look at her. A tomato."

"Even if she swore you were not at the theatre, it wouldn't help," Mandel told him, letting his eye wander curiously over Craig's face, the small mouth under the slight mustache, the tight eyes which shone or smoldered as Craig preferred. "I have another idea."

"You stay up nights thinking nasty things," Craig said, but he was suspicious now, clouding smoke deliberately through rounded lips.

"If she could account for you for the whole evening . . ." Mandel went on, "that's a different story."

"What's up. Get to the point. We're old friends."

"You'll be surprised," Mandel said. "Murder."

The nonchalance dissolved. Craig paled, butted his brows into one another. "You're crazy."

"Or you were," Mandel said.

"I never went in for murder," Craig said in sudden desperation. "I'm too smart. You know that."

"Oh, I'm surprised all right," Mandel admitted. "But this wasn't for money. Nothing like that."

"Who?" Craig asked. He seemed to cling to the wooden arm of the chair, to lean over it as though it were the rail of a jeopardized ship. "Who got killed?"

"A man who made it hot for a pal of yours a few years back," Mandel looked at him directly now, the dull eyes engaged hotly as on a target. "A priest." Craig looked shocked. "The priest who tipped us off about Martin Lynn. Father Kirkman."

Craig breathed heavily over the edge of the chair. His forgotten cigarette burned his fingers and he snapped it to the floor. "I'd forgotten him," Craig said. "I'd forgotten him completely."

"Do you want to tell the story and make it easy?"

"There is no story. This is ridiculous," Craig said, summoning up the old imitation of courage, the armor of his elan. "Positively ridiculous. I haven't seen that priest in five or six years."

"You mentioned Lynn yesterday; it took awhile for me to remember things. I had to check the records. It was all there."

"I'm innocent," Craig said and fumbled for a cigarette with nervous fingers. Never before had he been accused of a crime unjustly. He was like an actor who has played a scene many times easily and naturally on the stage, confronted with the same situation in life; the lines did not fit, the gestures were atrociously inadequate. The well-learned performance suddenly did not apply. "I'm innocent," he repeated, and thought—I sound exactly as though I'm lying.

3
The Word

THE GRIM detective, whose name was Evers, did most of the talking, but Martin found it difficult to concentrate on what he was saying. Evers had removed his coat and his muscular body strained through the white shirt; his sleeves were rolled back on hairy arms. The excitable detective, whose name was Lindell, sat on the arm of a chair against the wall. A stenographer, a small birdlike man with a green eyeshade, sat at Evers' right with a notebook and pencil, prepared to record his confession. Martin sat across a table from Evers, looking brightly into the detective's face, as though he were a promising student summoned for examination.

He was not frightened. He was conscious of a certain anticipation at the pattern events would fall into; but he was not fearful. He felt, above all, immeasurably relieved; it was relief that made it so difficult to listen to what Evers was saying, just as he had barely heard the questions they had put to him outside at the high desk where a policeman wrote in a large book with a harsh pen. His name, his age, something; he kept thinking that the tall cop was like a recording angel. The great thing was that he didn't have to worry anymore; the chase was over. He imagined his mother smiling, the old priest crowding his bulk happily back into the confessional. The high blank-walled room of his distress was less confining now; he could breathe in it. If the girl hadn't come along, he thought with joy, he might have done something else; he was grateful to her.

Evers cleared his throat loudly and artificially, laying his hands flat on the table and fixing Martin with what was intended to be a foreboding stare. Martin smiled at him. Had the detective spoken? Martin didn't want to be rude. Across the room he could see the bars outside the windows; they were on the first floor of the jail. There was, he knew, a policeman beyond the door. Back of them, deeper into the building, were the cells of prisoners, where the coldness would be also comfort. This room was high-ceilinged like the ghost room of his fears, but there were green blinds at the windows, faded and torn, some of them, and a naked-looking water-cooler in a corner. Refreshment—he thought with hazy joy. Peace.

"All right, Martin Lynn," Evers said. Martin wondered where Mandel was. Had the spare, listless detective known all the time—in the lobby, in the car? "Will you tell us," Evers said, "or will we tell you?"

How much could they know? He had left nothing behind; no tangible clues in the room—he was certain of that. Perhaps emotions were recorded in places: his anger smeared across the rug, his fear stained spottily on the wallpaper; his desperation chipped into the desk. The memory of the passions was now like a distant panorama, far off and vague. The film of the murder flickered mistily in his mind now; its clarity was blurred up; as though light had been let into the room and the projection on his brain washed out. He felt airy, freed of the burden of his own freedom; in the atmosphere of atonement.

"Then we'll tell you," Evers had apparently waited for his reply, and Martin smiled because he had forgot to answer. It couldn't have been the girl; she had not had time to betray him; they had been there in the doorway waiting for him. All evening, perhaps; while he was at Counihan's, while he was at the funeral home, as he talked to the girl and pursued the old lady, they had been waiting. It was easier now to think about it all; all the terrors were now only things that had happened, innocuous events fallen into insignificance; the occurrences of a day, explainable, reassuring, part of a pattern which was completed now that the sin was known. The echoes which had resounded along eternity had quieted down now. The terrible responsibility of confession had been removed from him. Never had he felt so sure of himself, as though he had found a place to belong here in the room at the jail with the squat, beefy, abrupt men who spoke at him in reverberant voices. One of them boomed away at him now in low, affable thunder. He must listen. He hoped his mother was smiling at him now.

". . . at ten o'clock exactly," Evers was saying. They didn't know so much after all; it had been earlier than that. He would have to tell them. He raised his hand to interrupt, but Evers had referred to a notebook and didn't see him. "The manager heard the shot and saw you as you ran out of the lobby. Since the cashier was shot from behind, she——"

The words faded away from Martin, hazed out to a

distance, like a bad telephone connection. They didn't know anything—not anything at all. With a grind, the film began again, flashing away on the clear, blank wall of the room from which there was no exit; his mother moaned and turned in the casket; the voices fluttered down again like birds round the confessional and the old priest peered evilly out at him. Nothing at all was over; nothing had come to an end. They had arrested him for the wrong crime.

He tried to concentrate on Evers' words, but they were entirely incomprehensible, like a foreign language. The room began to go round and round and he thought with a frantic joy—this will do it. I am coming apart at last; the mind clanks and pulls at the moorings; the memories will be scattered like flower petals on the water and I will be adrift on oblivion; no realization will be left. I will be blessed with insanity now.

But again it was only the body—the weak, weary body —that collapsed, sagging down between the table and the chair, reeling away from the words and the awful error. The old priest's face came nearer and nearer, enlarging like a balloon, a distortion of terror, so that he cried out in the room and created another echo before the two detectives got to his side. He watched the stenographer close his book with a sigh and put away the pencil, before he slid insensibly to the floor.

II

When Father Roth came off the altar after the nine o'clock Mass on Sunday morning he found the housekeeper waiting for him with a message. Mandel had called and wanted to be called back at the earliest opportunity. There were some ten minutes before the next Mass began, so he went off along the brick wall toward the rectory in his alb and cincture. All of the old pain and puzzle which had rendered him restless through the night came back to him, popping up through the peace and serenity the Mass had bestowed.

He traced once again the path of his decision in regard to the damaging slip of paper, rehearsed again to a skeptical, troubled segment of his mind the justice of his course. It was not, in the first place, definite proof of murder; but all his worry about it had not convinced him that it was no proof at all. He himself had taken the call from Mrs. Lally about the death of Martin's mother; there would have been no reason for Martin to call, either in person or by phone.

And if it were a clue left behind by Martin as murderer, there was yet justification for his withholding it from Mandel. Justice and mercy, under whatever disguises, were identical in the end, like twins at a masquerade. If he surrendered the paper to Mandel, he would be compelled to watch the wheels of an impersonal justice whirring and buzzing about the boy's head, drowning out forever, perhaps, prayer and repentance. By reserving the information to himself, he opened up a way back for the sinner; time might reassert in Martin the habit of honesty, of repentance, of confession habits he once, as a Catholic, had had.

Still, with all his repeated arguments, the priest was still haunted by the taciturn spectre of Mandel as he dialed the number of the detective bureau; he imagined the tall man shaking his head and fixing his lips primly when he found out. "It's too late now," Mandel might say patiently when the information finally came to him, and turn his mild eyes accusingly on the priest, implying: You, of all people, obstructing justice. And if the boy fled——?

The priest stood by the desk in the parlor, waiting for the connection to be made, while the Sunday sun streamed through the windows, picking out the cracks and warpings on the old boards. It might be any Sunday, with Father Kirkman and the usual visiting priest and himself looking forward to breakfast; only it wasn't; there were two visitors today and he would probably eat alone. He told himself stubbornly that Martin must be given a chance to admit the sin, to churn his will into motion, to return to the flock.

He finally got through various voices to Mandel. "I wanted to tell you," the detective said wearily through the mechanism. "They picked up Martin Lynn last night." The priest stiffened. "For robbery. It all happened before I knew it. They're holding him on suspicion for that Galaxy Theatre business; robbery and shooting. The cashier's gonna live, by the way. He's in a cell now. I thought— since he's in your parish—you'd like to know. . . ."

"Are you sure?" the priest asked. "Have they evidence?" The minor crime seemed incapable of explaining the fear, the distress in the boy; it certainly did not explain the slip of paper.

"It's all roundabout. And only suspicion," Mandel admitted. "But they got a lot of witnesses who said he'd been acting funny all day Saturday. He was seen near the theatre Friday night. Then he turned up at Swanson's with a lot of money and later at Counihan's; unusual for him. And he's scared all right."

"It's not possible," the priest said. "He couldn't have done that—" He almost said "too" and debated again within himself about the slip of paper.

"It's not a strong case," Mandel admitted.

"I'd be willing to vouch for his innocence on that charge," the priest said. The conviction came on him unaware; he could believe that Martin might kill in an access of grief, but robbery seemed too pale somehow.

"I'm not convinced," Mandel agreed, "myself. If you'd be responsible for him. . . ."

How far did the shepherd go for his sheep? If Martin were not worthy of trust. . . . If the grace did not arrive— like a letter gone astray— The line between mercy and foolishness was so narrow, so thin to limited sight. But the good shepherd went to foolish lengths.

"I'll be responsible," he told the detective. "I'll take a chance on him."

Mandel inserted a pause of acceptance. "When can you come?"

They arranged to meet at one o'clock at the city jail. "I'll be here," Mandel said. "Look me up. I'll take care of it."

"Martin—" Father Roth said. "If he wants to go to Mass— You have a chaplain here. Would you mention it to Martin?"

There was silence for a moment. "I already asked him," Mandel said wryly. "He didn't want to go."

"Oh." The sexton pulled on the ropes and the old metal of the church bells clanged. The priest hung up the phone and went back toward the sleepy pews to offer God to God. Irony was always present; he was willing to attest to Martin's innocence of robbery because he believed him guilty of murder. It was the feast of St. Hilarion, who was known as a conqueror of evil spirits; the priest said a prayer to him.

III

Martin was surprised to see that the windows contained not only bars, but wooden frames holding glass as well. He wondered why it had never occurred to him that protection against cold and rain was afforded prisoners; comforts for criminals, on no matter how primitive a basis, always seemed inconsistent with their punishment. The sinner exposed to the elements, chained to the rock, he had thought.

The frame was raised slightly from the sill now and a mild breeze nuzzled in. He could reach out and touch the bars themselves; they were cold and gritty and rusted; particles of dry metal came off on his hands. This was a disillusionment too; he had always pictured the confining bars as neatly and smoothly black, as in a painting. They had not, he reflected sadly, meant freedom for him after all. Even irony was not to be depended upon. Things turned out so differently, no matter with what precision you foresaw the shadowed events. Familiarity always evaded you in the end. He could have been exultant if the charge were murder, he thought. He would have been in a different part of the jail with the mark of Cain set clearly on him, the enormity of his offense buoying him up. He could have gone to Mass, taking comfort from the old mumble of words, from the candles, from watching the vestments whirl in the priest's wake as he turned from book to blessing.

Suppose he were convicted of robbery? Three months in jail? Six months? A year? He had no idea. Legal expiation for murder was more precise. He turned from the window and surveyed the room: the flat bed, the plain table, the chair, the implements of cleanliness. It's like a student's room, he thought, where a man is given time to study out himself, to pore over and over the one volume he should be familiar with.

If it should happen that way, could he apply the sentence against the crime which he had actually committed? Could he bind God with a bargain unknown to the law which imposed the punishment, saying daily to himself: this is my payment to Father Kirkman. They have put me here for one purpose, but I am adapting it to another. I'm doing my own suffering in my own way. Would it serve in the final records? But he knew it would not. You'd think they'd be smarter, he said to himself bitterly; you'd think they'd arrest the right man—and he sank onto the inflexible bed in weakness. Tears blurred on his lashes. The only sure way to receive his just punishment was to confess, to declare himself.

He saw again the high, blank room with the confessional boxes in it. They were permanent fixtures there now; he couldn't remember them when he had first invented the room. Now they were all around it, in every corner and along the bare white walls. "How long since your last confession?" a voice said hollowly, coming from nowhere in particular. It was as though all the wooden boxes had mouths where the curtains hung down and were speaking in chorus. "What have you done since then?" He remembered as a boy withholding a sin in confession; it was a minute, venial offense; but its suppression had increased his fervency on the admissible ones. It had been a hot summer afternoon and he had stood in the uneven line along the church wall, under the carvings of the Stations of the Cross, concealing the deed in his clasped hands. In the dark hold of the confessional, he kept wishing that the priest would accuse him of it—so he could simply say "Yes." It would have been so easy to agree, to nod, to say "That's true" almost as though it had been an oversight. It was less humiliating; it shared the sin somehow with the priest himself. "Oh yes, Father, I did that. Twice." Affirmative words, echoes of the real and terrible statement; like filling in the blank on a form. He was convinced that he would be utterly honest if it were a matter—right now—of looking down a printed list of sins and checking off Murder, Sacrilege. If he could just do that and hand it in and wait for an answer in the mail, like applying for a job. "In reply to yours of the third. . . ."

But he had wished for some such dispensation the last time and none had come. The priest had sat stoically, leaning his face on his fist, and waited for the humiliation. But Martin could not say it; the sin clove to the roof of his mouth, even though he thought, with great fear, that he could never entertain the Host while this unspoken sin tenanted his tongue. He had left the confessional in misery.

He had been fourteen then and terror racked at him until he devised a circuitous solution. He had gone home and eaten his dinner shakily and afterwards, in a corner of the hallway, to which he had fled with a pencil and a school notebook, he had written down in a trembling hand "I made a bad confession," and followed it with the sin and gone back to the church, in perspiration and fear, taking up his place in the line and pressing his message through the grill at the priest. The priest had had to switch on his light to read it and after he had turned it off again, Martin could only nod dumbly in the darkness, accepting his admonition and his penance in stricken silence. The spoken word which was the visible sign of his courage—the overt token of humility—he had been unable to form. He could not bear witness to himself.

Sitting now on the drab-blanketed bed, he wondered if he could follow the same procedure again, and he thought of asking the guard for writing material so he could tame his fear on the paper. But even as he considered it, the old priest's head loomed out at him, roughly exhorting him to face up to it. "Speak up, boy," the old priest said. And his mother joined in from her coffin: "Say it, Martin. Tell them." And he knew he could not, his tongue was tied securely with his own pride, his own shame, his inadequacy. It was going too far toward them, he thought. He could not be expected to make every concession. It's their job to find out—the priest's and the detective's. That's what they're for. He enjoyed a momentary image of Father Roth and Mandel stumping along behind bloodhounds and holding huge magnifying glasses in their hands and saying "hmmm" professionally. Let them come and get me, he thought stubbornly. And he lifted up his head and his defiance dried the tears on his cheeks and he looked up toward the splintered, cracked ceiling and repeated his prayer which was more like a challenge. "Come and get me," he said. It was the only way he could be sure of mercy.

Then the guard came and told him he was to be taken away. "Where?" he asked.

"St. Stephen's Rectory," the guard said. Martin could not rid himself of the thought that Father Kirkman had sent for him.

IV

The twelve o'clock Mass was still going on in the church when Father Roth received another call from Mandel. "I'm bringing Martin out," he said. "To the rectory. Along with another man—a man I suspect of the murder."

"Another man." The priest was stunned. "Another suspect?"

"Not another suspect. This is the first one. I want to talk to him in the study there. If you agree."

"Of course. Who is he?"

"Man named Craig," Mandel said. "You wouldn't know. He's got a record. The inquest comes up Tuesday and I want to test an idea."

"You said it was an amateur's job."

"That was a guess. The Conroy girl is coming over, too."

"Is it to be a—showdown?"

"You might call it that. I'm hoping for a confession. We ought to be there about one. In a few minutes."

"About Martin," the priest began.

"Yes?"

"Will he stay for the—showdown?"

"I hadn't thought. Should he?"

"It might—help," the priest said lamely and clipped off the conversation. The advent of another suspect confused him. Was the name on the paper accidental then? A ruse perhaps to throw suspicion toward the innocent? Was Martin Lynn, with his desperate, plaintive eyes, after all stricken only with loss of his mother? "It's as though you're arresting me," he had said to Mandel yesterday and there had been apprehension behind the surface jest. If Martin were present when Mandel made the attempt to unmask Craig, the truth might appear; Mandel might seek surrender from one quarter and get it from another. The priest was inclined to accept still the meagre evidence offered by the slip of paper; it was like a last word from Father Kirkman, a final message thrown over the wall of the grave—not merely to satisfy the demands of temporal justice, but to further the ends of God's love— to provide an opening for forgiveness.

The priest knew more now about the Lynns—from the simply accessible source of the walking parish archive— Mrs. Kelley, Mrs. Lally, the visitors to the rectory this morning. Mrs. Lynn had been a "devout Catholic"—they all agreed on that. This might mean nothing more than that she had served on sufficient pointless committees and made a satisfactory number of Sodality appearances. But it could also mean that she had been a genuine and fervent child of God, carrying her love to the ridiculous lengths that marriage and motherhod permit. The boy's father had been a petty gambler, a careless husband, a "bad

Catholic." Martin himself had abandoned the Church some years ago, at the time of his father's death. Before that he had been a timid student in the parish school and a shy altar boy. He had been rejected for military service because he was classified "psychoneurotic." The designation of this phrase was vague, both to the users of it and to himself; it might be applied to any number of aberrations or interpretations and none of the chattering women attributed abnormality—which they would have insinuated elaborately—to the boy. Mandel wanted reasons, the priest thought; there might be reasons in all this, somewhere—if he could find them. Or if the boy would find them for him.

Rita Conroy arrived then. The young priest wondered if she had attended Mass and tried to read evidence of devotion in her eyes; but the disguise was as complete and inscrutable as ever; the cosmetics question-marked her face, chalking over meanings.

"I don't know why Mandel wants me," she said, and stalked uneasily in the parlor under the Immaculate Conception. She spoke without emotion, as though she were immune to grief, passion, excitement. The young priest was reminded again of the peculiar asceticism of worldliness: the utter detachment from the spiritual.

"We'll all be here," he said to her. "The boy's coming, too."

"The boy?"

"Martin Lynn." It could have been any name for all the recognition it called up in her eyes.

"Is he—under suspicion?" she asked after a time.

"Not for—this," the priest said. "For something else. A robbery."

"A robbery," she said. "With his mother dead?"

The priest shrugged. A tatter of smile touched his lips which would have been sardonic in its entirety. "You suggested—murder."

She turned to look at him long and deliberately, the face as blank as a baby's. "I didn't suggest it."

"The possibility," he amended.

She stared for several minutes out of the front window. On the pavement a few early-leavers were trickling out from the last Mass, absenting themselves as unobtrusively as the words of the Last Gospel allowed: "He came to His own, and His own received Him not."

"Can you conceive," she asked finally, still with her back toward him, "of anyone wanting to kill a priest?"

"Oh, yes," he said. "Besides, we have proof. We don't have to guess at that."

"Not as a man," she said. "As a priest. Just as a priest. Because he is a priest?"

"Of course. We remind people of too many things." He talked at her back. "Of God; and heaven; even of hell. Fear might do it. Because of that. Or jealousy; because we have what we have. We've climbed Mount Tabor. Or anger at God himself. Because we're handy and He is not."

She listened still without turning. "Or because," he said slowly, "because we are bad priests. That might happen too. Priests are sometimes unworthy." It was, he thought, a comforting truth for the skeptical.

"Often, I'll bet." It was said in bitterness, in retaliation.

"Too often," he admitted. "But not so often as you might think." He thought of his own temptations; the scruple and the liberal interpretation, self-righteousness and charity, the pride that was hidden in humility. It was so difficult to distinguish, sometimes, between the marauder in the garden at night, whom you must suffer, and the money changer in the temple by day whom you could not abide. "The devil has special traps for us. Only God can lead us around them." Life was an obstacle course where the hurdles were always being changed. "But God can sustain us—or forgive—anything." He envied the apostles the gift of tongues again; it was needed now in a new way; not to cross the barrier of language, but the barrier of atmosphere, of associations. The truth had become the vapid truism to the skeptical ear. Salvation . . . charity . . . paradise—the revival meeting had ground the cross to sawdust.

"I do hope he isn't long," she said suddenly as though they were waiting for an unpunctual friend on a social occasion. "It's such a cold room."

V

Martin had been placed in a police car with Evers and a uniformed man. They followed another car, containing a group of persons he did not get a chance to observe, to the rectory. Why there? Why, also, was Father Roth willing to attest to his innocence until the evidence was more conclusive, as Evers had said. Nobody could be sure he had not held up the theatre; nobody had watched his movements that evening. Unless—the possibility struck him like a blow—there was someone who knew he had committed the murder. The woman with the squeaky voice? He saw her again in the darkness with the shadows of the branches across her face. I should have done it, I should have done it then, he told himself. But if she knew, she would have told Mandel—she wasn't the type to keep it to herself—and he would not have been allowed to leave the jail. The girl then? He could not believe that she would betray him; they were friends. He thought with exultance that perhaps Mandel had found something— some tangible clue to chain him to his crime—and was arranging a confrontation. Let them figure it out, he breathed intensely; let them figure it out, God. Let them free me that way. And he was only vaguely troubled by the alternatives; freedom from punishment or freedom from guilt. Above all he wanted the film to shut off inside his head.

They arrived at the rectory at a bad time. The last Mass was over and the parishioners were all over the sidewalks, streaming down from the church doors. Mandel stood on the sidewalk, his thinness carrying his embarrassment above the Sunday hats. He looked around tentatively as though he himself were a bystander, gawking at the police and their charges. Martin saw a policeman and a man in street clothes hustle up the steps to the rectory, and then he and Evers alighted from the car and were themselves crosscutting through the mob of Catholics, who clustered in small advantageous groups of curiosity, buzzing with comment on the police cars and their occupants.

The same old thing, Martin thought; gossip swallowing up the grace; you could see it in their eyes. Heads wagged together, shocked whispers hissed toward him; smug pronouncements stabbed at his ears as Evers propelled him across the pavement and up the curved stone steps. Out practicing their charity, his bitterness interrupted for a moment his own apprehension of what was to happen inside; the ordinary, fearful Catholics, he thought, following the faded pattern of self-respect, mediocrity, busily going about everybody's business. They were the sheep, bound and gagged, and seeking willingly the slaughter.

His anger had entranced him more than he knew. He had moved with Evers to the top of the steps, absorbed in his resentment, and now he could see the vestibule doors flung open before him and the uncarpeted hallway beyond. The parlor was just a few steps from him.

He stopped abruptly in the doorway and clutched automatically at the frame as his head spun and clouded and lightened; realization eddied round him like water: here he had killed the old priest; this was the scene of the crime.

"You sick?" Evers said to him.

It was just a matter of holding on, of seeing it through. The body of the old man was not there now; heaven knew it had popped up in enough places since for him to be sure of that; it had a way of getting around. And there could be no menace in the stiff furnishings. He remembered the desk and the high-hung painting and the fireplace. They wanted him to blanch, to betray himself; to succumb to the hand which tightened now in his viscera. That's what they wanted. They thought he would

scare at the sight and spill out everything. Bringing him
back was a trick, he told himself craftily; he should have
known. They wanted to shock him into confession; it was
a part of the conspiracy of the old gray head peering out
from the curtains and beckoning at him, coaxing him to
the grill. But he'd show them.

"Nothing's wrong." He tried to flavor it with surprise.
He started to move. But it was just as it had been when
he wanted to run from the corpse in Murray's basement;
a thick viscosity hugged around him. Each step required
a separate effort, an individual dispatching of messages
from his brain to his muscles. His progress along the corridor to the parlor door seemed to him jerky, spasmodic,
eternally prolonged. It was a fatal door all right, he thought
when he saw it, when he struggled over the threshold;
he must see that it didn't become fatal to him again. His
courage wavered now that he had actually got to the
door and he turned his head away quite involuntarily,
not wanting to look directly into its depth. But he saw
Mandel behind him and knew it was no time to surrender
to the stubborn body and the aching brain. With an effort
of will, he turned his head back, forced his eyes to focus
toward the objects in the room. He saw only the upflung
eyes of the figures in the Immaculate Conception painting
and dropped his head, bowing it before this shrine of his
guilt. It would be better not to go in with head up; there
were too many accusing objects. And then he remembered the crucifix. It was as though his fear had held it
so close to him that its outlines had become blurred and
forgotten. It would be on the desk, turned away from him.
He would have to avoid that, above all things.

He was aware of voices and people to his right, up near the front windows. Keeping his head bowed, he edged into the room, his eyes on the carpet, his hands clenched— they felt enormous again, disproportionate, monstrous. He was aware of a labored, asthmatic breathing. In one corner of his eye he could see the bottom edge of the desk along a carpet and he cowered away from it. He could, he decided, go over by the fireplace, over into the angle made by the bricks and the wall; there he would be tempted less to stare at the crucifix, at the witnesses of his sin. It was almost as though the crucifix—the figure on it—stretched out a restraining hand as he passed, asking acknowledgment, pleading for recognition like a spurned friend. But he had got past it at last, was standing in the corner which was almost an alcove, out of range of the miniature of awe. He was safe now—safe until some other horror was sprung at him. He didn't know what tricks they mightn't try.

He saw the young priest then, standing solemnly by the windows; and the girl, cross-legged and remote on a straight wooden chair, watching the others—not him, at least—dispassionately, as though it all had nothing to do with her.

The girl! he thought wildly. She's the one, she's told the priest what I said last night—and about my following the woman. That's how he knows. But they were both looking toward the door, toward Mandel, who had just entered, and they were not—it appeared—even interested in him. Then the young priest turned toward him and smiled; it was a slight smile, but undeniable. He tried to smile back, thinking there was no rational answer to this

224

whole elaborate plot. Their strategy was impenetrable. Like God's.

And then he saw Craig, who must have been the other prisoner. Certainly he looked like a prisoner: he was a different Craig—soiled, rumpled, taut, puffing violently at a limp, flattened bit of cigarette. He sat in a chair opposite Martin, and he was by no means smiling and secure.

"Mr. Craig," Martin breathed at him. And the grim eyes flicked toward him and regarded him with belligerence. Craig came as a shock to Martin—this Craig at any rate. Another symbol of his own possible future was shattered before his eyes. Could nobody, he asked himself, bear the burden of guilt? live comfortably in the catacombs of rebellion away from the smug, prescribed attitudes? Not his father certainly; and not the girl; and not even Craig, apparently, who had seemed the most secure of them all. And what connection could there be between Craig and the robbery and the rectory?

Mandel was closing the door methodically, turning the knob and testing the catch carefully before he turned back to face the people in the room.

Martin felt he could understand nothing; it all seemed a complicated tissue of machinations designed only to break down his will; a conspiracy of the mediocre people. Were all the disparate elements of his own night of terror brought together here solely to frighten him, or was there another, deeper affinity among them all, some slim needle of circumstance stitching them all together—the priest, the girl, Craig and Evers—and Mandel, who stood now looking over them uneasily. There was menace in it somewhere; they were all, in some sense, minions of the old priest, acting out patterns he would have approved. But it seemed unlike Craig, unlike the girl to rope him round like this. And the priest, who had seemed to be on his side—was he enemy or friend? Only Mandel was declared; he was enemy; his quiet face led on to doom of some kind. If only, Martin thought, he could trust the room not to betray him. He had forgotten for the moment his eagerness to be accused and thought only, instinctively, of avoiding capture. And in his preoccupation, he had relaxed his guard and the crucifix hailed him.

From his position left of the fireplace, he could see it clearly, standing delicately on the desk, exactly where it had been the last time he had seen it—had placed it there. It was oblivious of him; it did nothing, was immobile and bronze only. You could point me out, he said to it; you could settle the whole thing. And at the same time he feared that it would. But nothing happened. The figurine bore not witness, was only a slim, rounded doll of suffering on a flat cross done neatly into metal; the arms out, the head bent, the convex crown of the head meticulous among the formal thorns.

Mandel was mumbling to Evers at the door; Craig lit another cigarette. Martin's jaw tensed in a kind of interior smile as he stared at the crucifix. He had been pretty clever after all; he had been better than he thought. Since the figurine had not been moved, he felt sure it was not suspected as a weapon; he reflected that his accomplice in this crime was certainly beyond suspicion. He peered at it guardedly, attempting to distinguish on its surface any disturbing shade, any tinge of color which was not its

own. He could see nothing. Perhaps there was no reason
to worry at all; perhaps he could brazen through the whole
thing to a real freedom, succeed where his father and
Craig and the girl had failed, could go the entire way toward the bitter peace of evil.

But the dream was blurred again by its opposite; by
the weight of guilt, by the size of his hands, the terror in
the theatre lobby, the whirling confessionals and the old
priest's head. If he had been too clever, his peace, his refreshment might be postponed forever. Which release
promised the truer freedom?

"You'll want to know what all this is," Mandel addressed
them all shyly. It was like a business conference of agents
from far parts of the country. The detective stood at the
far side of Father Kirkman's desk, near the door, away
from them all. A round, faded Raphael mother and child
dotted his height.

"It's about the murder, of course." Craig twitched in
his chair. The girl shifted slightly, the handles on her bag
rattling. The murder, Martin thought; perhaps, after all . . .
"If the procedure is unusual, so is the case. . . ." Mandel
murmured on. Martin looked at the girl and stretched his
lips in a half-smile; there had been fellowship between
them last night. What had she done or said since? What
would she do now? But she seemed not to see him and his
eyes passed on to Craig, who sat miserably, slumped, under a dark rendering of the Crucifixion, in which the pale
Body was highlighted in the center of the rectangular
frame against a background of sneering faces. ". . . the
man under suspicion," Mandel paused. Will he name me,
thought Martin. But he didn't. "John Travis Craig."

Martin could not believe it. Craig and Father Kirkman. Craig under suspicion of his own crime, his own private crime. He looked at the man who had been his father's friend, his friend on Friday night. Craig sat still dejectedly, biting at a cigarette. Could this be a trap, still?

"Oh, Martin," Mandel sounded surprised. "I'd forgotten." His eyes wandered over the ceiling. "I meant to . . ." his voice trailed off and he looked at all of them apologetically. "This boy," he waved a loose gesture, "we had arrested for robbery. Something else entirely. On suspicion only, however. Father Roth has upheld his innocence. We're willing to free him on that word."

Is this charity, thought Martin? Pity? A trick? He was aware of Craig cracking his knuckles.

"You can go, Martin," Mandel said. "You're free."

The detective stared benignly at him across the crucifix, under the mother and child who had a joyful, swirling look. Martin tried to speak. Oh, I'm guilty all right, he presented the words to himself as invitingly as he could, I'm guilty of murder. I could save you time. But the words were rejected. He sat only, frigidly on the chair in the priest's study, in the circle of eyes and wondered if the rest of them could smell blood in the room as he could. Mandel continued to smile. Martin was aware of the priest's eyes on him, of the girl's, of a move from Craig— a sudden, jerky adjustment of the body in the chair. Craig was no longer a promise, an ideal. "Do you hear," Mandel repeated. "You're free."

If I leave, Martin thought, I'll never be free again. Where should I go? I got out that door once into the cold, uncomfortable night. If I go out again, I'll never get back in. It was home to him; he was being evicted from home and hope.

"I'll wait," he said finally, and the words sounded artificial; it was as though he were telling a lie. "I'll wait . . . and see."

"Very well," said Mandel. "After all, the old priest was your mother's friend." Martin thought of his mother lying upstairs at Murray's. Father Kirkman's money would bury her now; he had accomplished that. He remembered his promise of the night before; it had been so glib, so easy to promise surrender. But he was tired of running now. It seemed unfair to torture Craig with his guilt. The girl will speak now—she will not see an innocent man charged with this; she will speak, Martin thought, and I will be glad. I'll be free that way. The crucifix cannot speak but she will speak; she is my friend.

"The problem," Mandel said, "was always motive. Why should anybody want to kill Father Kirkman? So I went after a reason; I thought that would settle everything." The girl was listening intently; did he detect perspiration on the priest's brow? "I went back through the records; all Friday night. I haven't slept . . . to speak of . . . since Thursday." He grinned bleakly at them as though the personal note lightened the situation. "I remembered the Martin Lynn case." Martin felt the resentment rise; but weariness urged him to resignation; he had not the strength to hate anything now, and the column of ire subsided slowly. "Strange you should be mixed up," Mandel pointed a hand at Martin. "But there it is. Life. We share everything." Martin could not understand how his father fitted here. Father Kirkman had refused to bury the suicide, but he could not conceive Craig nurturing revenge for this; it was a defection outside his code. Still, there was so much beneath the surface: God bores like a chigger underneath the skin, biding His time.

Mandel went on as though he were reciting an ill-learned lesson, hesitantly. "I checked back. Looked up the man who handled the case. Your father—you knew he was a gambler, I guess, not always an honest gambler— if gamblers are ever honest. He'd got himself into a hole." Mandel sounded sympathetic, as though to be caught in panic between honesty and sin were a familiar dilemma. "He embezzled a pretty large sum from a man he was working for at the time; Father Kirkman had persuaded the man to give your father the job. Then Father Kirkman threatened to expose your father unless he gave himself up." Mandel looked out at them with compassion. "He couldn't bring himself to confess."

Martin dug down through the layers of memory, seeing how the song had gone out of his father's voice, how the laughter had run heavy and forced through the two narrow rooms. His father, too, had balanced on the brink of despair, fumbling to find words of humility among the inflexible phrases of pride. His father had at least had a promise of betrayal; he had not even that. Where the young priest and the girl were silent, Father Kirkman would have spoken.

"Craig here," Mandel was saying, "I got a quotation— the witness is still living—Craig said he'd kill the priest if he got a chance." Craig pressed a fist into the palm of a hand, holding on. "This was the chance. He thought about it a long time—all through the war, I suppose—and finally the chance came."

Craig slid to the edge of his chair, tremblingly. "It's all so long ago. Why would I kill him now?"

"Revenge," Mandel said, as though rendering a definition, "doesn't count time. It waits forever."

"For God's sake," Craig wept up at him, leaning forward from the chair, threatening to fall to his knees. "Believe me, it's not true. I wouldn't kill . . . anybody."

Martin thought: this is why my mother prayed; not only the gleaming men in sports coats; not only the wretched, wasted days in the grandstand or over the fight results on ticker tape—but this, too. She had been his father's conscience, bearing a borrowed load, tramping up the aisle between the confessionals with her doomed supplications. It was strange to think Mandel suspected Craig of killing the priest out of devotion to his father. Only of course Craig hadn't laid down anybody's life for his friend. The girl will have to speak now, he told himself with relief; she can't be that callous. He envied her the faculty of words, the freedom to weld truth into negotiable coin.

"Friday night," Mandel went on, still casually, "Craig came here to accomplish this. He must have watched his chance when everybody was out. He had been a Catholic once and probably knew the layout—although in any case, it was no trick to find out when the old man was alone. We have a witness for this." Craig stared at him with imploring eyes. Mandel gestured toward the door and Evers went out in search of the witness.

There couldn't, of course, be anybody, Martin knew.

It was all a mistake. The truth would come out now; he wondered if this calmness, this numbness, could maintain through climax and revelation; if he could withstand the final discovery. Someone was staring at him now and he brought his head around slowly to find himself confronted by the eyes of both the girl and the priest; they looked at him expectantly, half in horror. The girl has told the priest, he thought; they both know now. The girl's smooth brow was wrinkled delicately in a question, an invitation; the priest's cherubic face appeared to plead at him, saying that now was the time. He divined gradually out of the twin looks, which were fixed on him in beseeching urgency, that they expected him to speak; they were waiting for him to make the move. He tried to smile at them, but he could not.

When the witness came in, it turned out to be the woman with the scratchy voice. She came in, peering at them all nearsightedly, like a tourist in an art gallery. Martin saw the girl's hand clench; the expression which crossed the priest's face like a shadow looked very much like relief. This was the witness, then, who had watched him approach to murder from across the street. Craig needn't have worried; it would be all right.

She stood, swiveling her head from one to the other, back and forth between Martin and Craig. The boy had not seen her face clearly before; she had been condemned solely on the evidence of her voice. Now he fancied he detected kindliness in the sharp features, in the thin neck which rose out of her collar like a bird's: a kind of stupid benevolence. Mandel hovered behind her like a nervous parent displaying a clever child.

A croak of triumph came from her finally. "It's him," she said. "He's the one. I'm sure of it." And the bony finger leveled at Craig.

"It's a lie . . . a lie," Craig shouted. "You planted her. It's a frame." He writhed in the chair as though he were bound.

"A guilty man," the woman said, "if ever I saw one. He rang the bell and looked in the window and came in. Even with my eyes . . ."

Evers moved to Craig's side to quiet him with menace. Mandel led the woman from the room, but she chattered back over her shoulder at the young priest until she was out of sight. "A blessing I should be watching, Father," she said. "Why, I rarely go near the window. . . ." Mandel closed the door on her.

The girl leaned in toward Martin quickly, her perfume looping sweetly around him. "You won't let this go on, will you?" she breathed urgently. "You can't." But he only looked at her wonderingly, thinking, she's nervous. She can't stand the waiting either. But it's plain that she knows. Why doesn't *she* tell?

"There's that then," Mandel said to Craig. "You were seen."

"Couldn't have been . . . couldn't have been," Craig strung himself to his feet unsteadily. "Mandel. I'm innocent. I have proof. I'll tell the truth."

Martin wondered if Craig would wheel around and accuse him. He waited hungrily for the pointing finger and the outraged declaration.

"I couldn't have been here," Craig said. "I was—" his

hysteria seemed to die away, "—at the Galaxy Theatre. I pulled that job. I shot the girl and took the money."

Evers' head bobbed up. Martin looked squarely at the young priest in dismay. The cherubic face pleaded with him still, exhorting confession; he and Father Kirkman were side by side, like faces in a musical revue, sharing exact expressions, urging him on—as though he were losing a race. He tried to dispatch messages from his eyes; I need help, he tried to say. Expose me. But the priest only looked.

"It makes sense," Evers said to Mandel. "It's more like him."

"Why, the boy'll tell you," Craig pointed at Martin. It was the accusing finger, but with the wrong significance. "I saw him that night; I gave him money. I—" Craig faltered at his own confession, "—I thought I could frame him with it. I knew you'd be looking for me and I thought it would throw you off the track if he had the money. I didn't plan on—all this."

But Mandel was impassive. "Old cagey Craig," he said. "Just because the boy here's been cleared of the robbery, you'd assume it, would you?"

Craig's eyes grew large with shock. "It's true, I tell you. True."

"Frame me," Martin mumbled. It explained the visit, the money, the kindness in the darkness, the hope among the debris. There was nobody you could count on anywhere.

"Who wouldn't prefer a robbery charge to murder," Mandel said.

"You don't believe me," Craig said blankly, and sat down.

"It's open and shut," Mandel said, and was striding toward the desk, toward the crucifix. "Clear as day. You have the motive; you had the opportunity. You were seen." He had turned now and was coming back with something in his hands. "You even had the weapon," he said and brandished the crucifix over Craig's upturned, frightened face.

Martin was in the blank room now, guarded by his guilt. "Why don't You give me away?" he prayed plaintively.

"You struck the old priest with this," Mandel said brutally, popping his words out sharply. "You struck him in a fit of anger born out of revenge. You hit him over the head Friday night with this crucifix. Why don't you admit it?" The tall Jewish detective held the figurine delicately by the base, at an angle, bringing Craig face to face with his God.

Martin watched in fascination, his gaze locked on the bronze statue; he remembered how it felt against his hand, the sharp edges and the roundnesses; he remembered the jolt as it hit the priest; and the rasp as he rubbed it viciously to remove the blood. Why must they badger poor Craig? he thought. And he prayed that he would have the strength to speak himself, to tell the truth at this long last so intolerably overdue. But his lips were puffed and numb and said nothing.

"Please," Craig said in agony and covered his face with his hands.

"You see why," Mandel said, with abrupt kindness. "It's all plain now. You see why you're under arrest."

Martin heard from what seemed a long way off the sound of sobbing. It began as a series of throaty noises and coupled imperceptibly into a drawn grating sigh; it was like an animal crying lonesomely in a dark place. It inhaled desperately and gaspingly and then wailed out in a tangled, strangled monotone of hysteria. It's me—he thought hopefully—and I'm going mercifully mad. Mandel said curtly: "Take him out, Evers. He's breaking up." And he looked up and it was Craig crying after all, broken and bent and repentant before the crucifix.

Evers summoned a policeman and together they bundled Craig to his feet; they supported him on each side and gave the impression, as they guided him toward the door, that they were holding him together. He was like a scarecrow that has come unstuffed.

Mandel turned to the priest, holding out the crucifix. "I'm sorry about this, Father," he said. "No disrespect meant. But this was the weapon." He thought. "I'm sure. We found traces of blood." The girl seemed to shrink inside her shoulders.

The priest reached out and took the crucifix wordlessly.

"We checked it the first night, took specimens. No doubt about it." Mandel began to make notes in his book. "We'll have trouble getting a conviction. But his record's against him."

Martin stared at the three of them, stared from the frozen extremity of his own isolation. They didn't know, after all, he thought; they could not be so cruel as to stand by while Craig suffered—while he himself suffered. Not if they knew. They wouldn't hold their tongues if they knew, while he squirmed and battled on the chair. Even Judas had been granted accusation. "It is one of the twelve. . . ." But he was abandoned to his own will, marooned with the ghost of his indecision. It would be so simple for them; not even a word; maybe a gesture would do it. But they were silent, the priest and the girl, staring with a kind of reverent horror at the model of Christ crucified. He remembered that Peter had denied too: "I know not the Man." Oh, he had precedent all right. But the will and the word passed like strangers in the darkness.

He stood up at last and spoke to them, but they were not the words he longed to say. The horror could not be expressed, after all. "I'm going," he said and was surprised at the level, unemotional tone that issued from him. "To my mother." And he went lonesomely out of the room and down the steps and away along the drab streets. It was as though he had been left alone at night on the planks of a deserted railway station with all the lights out and the people gone and the last train hooting derisively in the distance.

VI

"Here," the priest said, and thrust the crumpled slip of paper into Mandel's hand. "It's from the pad. On the desk. The boy's name. Father Kirkman's writing."

The detective looked at it without comprehension. "It's a name and a phone number," he said, and the priest explained. Mandel turned it in the light until the indentations were clear to him. "Martin Lynn," he read hollowly and looked up with surprise.

"I thought," the priest said, "he would confess. Not so much to you, as to me."

"I knew Craig hadn't done it," Mandel said suddenly.

"He did the other thing, all right." Outside the police cars were rumbling away.

"But the records . . . the threat to revenge."

"It's all true. Only he didn't carry the revenge out. I expected a confession, all right. But not from the boy—" And he looked down at the girl who had not risen from her chair but had instead bowed her perkily-hatted head into her red-tipped hands and was weeping. "This won't help much to get a conviction," Mandel said, fingering the paper. "But we'd better go after him." He started toward the door.

"I would've told you yesterday," the priest said in apology. "Only it was slim evidence. And I hoped . . ." his eyes roved out the window, dull with disappointment, ". . . there might be repentance."

"There's more," the girl said quickly and looked up at them through the marks of her tears. "He followed that woman last night. He was threatening her. He thought she knew."

"Worse than I thought," Mandel said from the doorway. "Funny thing. The old lady's blind as a bat. She might have pointed at me." He smiled the bleak smile. "We'd better go armed, I guess. To a funeral home. It seems silly." He stared at the chair the boy had occupied. "But if this didn't break him down, he's a bad one. A real killer."

"He's not a killer," the girl burst out suddenly. "Not that way. He just—did it." She looked from one to the other, justifying the heedless action, the spurt of sin along the veins. "That's what he told me. I know how he felt." She thought fondly of what solace lay in the sin stated succinctly in law; the boy didn't have it so bad after all. "I guess he couldn't—say it," she added weakly.

Mandel put his hat awkwardly on his head. "Looks like everybody knew about this but me,"—he smiled the bleak smile again and went out. The priest replaced the crucifix softly on the desk, left it facing the girl, and followed.

VII

Martin sat by his mother, watching the daylight sieve through the blinds and whiten her face. He was conscious of nothing beyond the moment and the corpse; even the blank room in his brain had dissolved—the confessional no longer threatened. He was numb and exhausted and the screen of his mind was wiped clean; it was as though his mother were the active, feeling one and he the shell. Nothing moved in him at all, not fear, not pity, not anger or remorse. He was an insensible rock round which the waters raged. Will had been syphoned off from him; as a punishment, he thought, because he had not made use of it. He had had his cake and not eaten it, which was the ultimate sin and now he had been deprived. He was like a bombed house in the newsreels—the insides splintered and the walls standing. All his sensations were delayed; he could look at the wreath—Swanson had sent it after all —but time elapsed before it really nudged his conscious-ness; he could look at his mother but he recorded the sight seconds later. As a man can be seen chopping wood at a distance silently, until the wind brings the crack of the axe along tardily, the impression succeeded the event.

239

The time was gone; he had not declared himself at the moment when it was demanded. Not his own honesty or pity for Craig could move him. Even the crucifix had left him dumb. He thought how his father must have climbed the arch of the bridge, going like a sleep-walker toward the parapet, hoping for comfort among the waters. He wondered with a kind of relaxed interest how it would feel to step off into space jerked swiftly upward past the feet; the rush of wind against the jawbone, dusting at the eyes, and then the slapping impact of the water and the gobbling before the silence. He doubted if he would resist even for a frantic, instinctive second; he tried to piece out differences between living and dying and could discover no tangibles.

Swanson's wreath was the only floral offering; the casket looked cheap and dowdy in comparison with the bronze handles and thick, padded walls of the one which held the old priest downstairs. He had brought his mother no pomp. She would go into her fragile container, unspectacularly into the ground reserved for the poor—thinly separated from the carnivorous earth and the eager worms. There would be no protection for her. Father Roth might say a Mass, but it was not like the rich who were remembered week after week in the sonorous Sunday announcements. He had been able to give her only an unavailing stubbornness and reckless stupidity. He thought vaguely—but without energy—that he would like to crawl in beside the cold, resisting body, inch himself down against the bone and the chemicals and close the lid of the casket and share the poverty of death with her as well.

But someone stood in the doorway and he could not

be sure how long there had been another presence in the room. He looked languidly at a plump and elderly man, rather primly tucked into a dark suit, who stood respectfully in the doorway. His hair was plastered down with such stiffness that it appeared wildly unnatural. His eyes were slits which had been squinted by straining against the sun and his bushy eyebrows overhung them heavily, untidily; the face was dark from wind and weather but with a bright bronzing, and the ruts of expression were like intricate designs.

"Mrs. Lynn?" he asked in a low voice. Martin nodded. He thought it another friend of his father, but he could stir no interest. The man crossed the carpet and knelt on the prie-dieu. He was short and broad and moved with surprising grace. He crossed himself and contributed a series of hard, breathy prayers over the body, then crossed himself again, raised his head and stared frankly into the dead face of Mrs. Lynn. After a while he nodded his head slightly as though in affirmation, as though assuring Mrs. Lynn of something.

"Are you the family?" He turned to Martin, and the boy nodded dumbly, thinking what a curious word it was to apply to him; a collective designation of his solitary function. He was all the relatives, all the mourners, carrying out to the end the deprivation of his mother's life.

"You can be proud," the man said. "A good woman."

Not a friend of his father's, Martin thought; there was too much authority. "It shows. It comes out."

Martin looked dully at his mother, trying to find the traces of virtue which the man had read. He could see the peace that had replaced the weariness; nothing more.

Perhaps he had become accustomed to it; it was possible for familiarity to breed contempt even for goodness. He tried to pry a pristine impression out of the face he knew better than his own.

"Some of them," the old man went on, "you can tell they've been fighting it every inch, hanging on to life. Here there's goodness and peace."

"Who are you?" Curiosity came stumbling first through the fog of his numbness.

"A pallbearer," the man said. "A paid pallbearer." He said it quite proudly, as another man might lay claim to a difficult art. "But I have preferences. I don't carry anybody. I always look at the subject first."

"You do it often?"

"Often," the man said. "As often as there's a suitable subject. Some of these fellows," he said with disgust, "they'll carry anybody. They don't care who's inside." He snorted, then looked again toward Martin's mother. "Here: anybody can see. Class. I'll come cheerily tomorrow morning. Meaning no disrespect, of course."

"Class," Martin looked in amazement at the dead face.

"It's plain," the old man said. He wheezed after prolonged conversation, his syllables shared breath with a whistle now. "I turned down a man this morning. Not like her."

"Class," Martin said speculatively. "Was he rich?"

"A wealthy man," the old fellow snorted. "You should have seen the trappings, like a Pharaoh. But I told them. I don't come to just anybody."

Martin stared at the corpse, attempting to recreate on the worn-out features the separate virtues his mother had practiced. She had loved all right—if that was class; through thick and thin, rain or shine, good or bad, clear up to the edge of the grave. She had loved, all right; it had been humiliating but she had loved. And she had refreshment, light, peace—class, the man said.

"Why, I'll be happy to accept this job," the man said. "A decent funeral." The lines around the eyes threatened a smile, but its consummation was restrained by circumstances, by his calling. He bowed solemnly toward the casket and turned to go.

Martin thought: nothing I did mattered anyway; the burial would be the best possible after all because of the subject. There had been glory round the brass bed and he had not seen it in the darkness. He was absorbed then in regret so that he did not hear the rattle of heels on the stairs—not for a moment. Remorse muffled up sounds so that he was not prepared for the girl when she ran breathlessly into the room. She looked questioningly after the old man. "Was he . . . police?" she said.

"Oh, no," Martin said and was amazed at his calm; how little of turmoil carried through into the world outside the head!

Rita glanced furtively at the casket before she went on: "They're coming," she told him. "They're on their way. They know."

"They know." He repeated it hollowly and knew no elation. He had not confessed; his courage had been sparse to the end; he could not match the nobility in the casket beside him.

"Aren't you going to go? To run?"

"Where should I go?"

"Anywhere. Away. If it's money—" She reached toward the clasp of her bag.

"Money," he said, and there was only emptiness in the pronouncement.

"But you have a chance," she said. "I know why you did it. I can understand. I'd have done it myself."

He smiled at her benignly. It was as though he were the adult and she the child; he the rich and she the poor. "I can't understand now, myself," he said. "It did no good." He thought of the voices churning down around the confessional. "Father Kirkman was right. There's nothing I could do for my mother—not like that."

"He was never right," she said in a furious whisper. "You said yourself he had power. He was the Church. I hate it, too."

He looked at her for a long time. She was only a nervous, jittering girl after all. Like Craig, she lost her mask at crucial times. Now the slick, shiny exterior had peeled away, like a fashion advertisement in an old, yellowing magazine; the glamor had departed. "You're funny," he said and remembered the First Communion photograph. She had been with him all the way; she had been an ally, but not a goal. He had been trying to escape into her world, and she was with him all the time; in the same boat. "I wanted to confess," he said, "but I couldn't. I wasn't strong." A faint spark of the old resentment spluttered inside him. "Why didn't you tell them back there in the rectory? Why didn't you tell?"

"I was afraid," she said in a voice suddenly small. "I was glad—you'd done it. I'm guilty, too."

He felt pity for her. They had come through it all to-

gether. "It's all right now," he said. "You can be forgiven."
Sin isn't proud, he thought. It will live anywhere; it had
roosted beside them both with its obscene beak and filthy
feathers, pecking into their hearts. "Look at my mother.
Why, she loved me. Love is so . . . ridiculous." He said it
lovingly, as a father indulgently reproves his child.

They could hear voices and a clatter of feet downstairs.
The girl started: "They've come after you," she said
quickly, though not so quickly as before. Some of the urgency had gone out of her. "They're armed. They think
you're a killer. They think you're not well."

"Not well," he repeated. He remembered the psychiatrist cocking his head in surprise behind the flat desk.
"Don't you go out with girls?" the psychiatrist had said.
And the draft card had burned in his pocket thereafter, a
symbol of his shame, of his slavery to outmoded moral
codes. He stared brightly at the girl. "That's what I
thought, too," he said. "But I was wrong."

The noises below increased in volume. He thought he
could hear Albert's scandalized voice trying to restrain
the police. "Why, I couldn't even go crazy," he said. "I
wanted to and I couldn't." He looked fondly at the casket
and its cold occupant. "Why, there isn't time," he said abruptly. "There are so many people to hate. There's not
time." Below the stairs a voice tried to whisper and shout
at the same time. They would come to accuse him now;
he had his wish.

"You stay here with my mother," he said, with sudden
authority. "You don't want to go through what I've been
through."

"You'd better not go down," she told him.

"There's nowhere else to go. I'll welcome them." He would be like a host going down to greet his guests. He was aware that the girl was looking at him incredulously and with disgust; the old scorn foaming up at him again. He was betraying her, conforming where the new dispensation of freedom demanded revolt. They had been allies and now he was abandoning the post; fluttering a white flag and leaving her alone behind the gaudy parapet.

"It's the only way," he said. "I'm not strong enough. Nobody can resist forever."

And he remembered all at once that there was still a choice to make, an action he could perform. The confessional still hunched in the church; there was still something he could declare. He could own up to everything, bowing down before a severer detector than Mandel. "Kill the Church," he said to the girl, scornfully. "Why, it would take a massacre—one priest after another." He thought of the crucifix. "They'd just go on suffering." He started for the door. "Like Christ."

"Watch out," she called to him. "Be careful."

But he went boldly down the steps, toward the circle of men who huddled at the foot, Mandel towering above them all. Martin was faintly aware of a glint of light on metal.

"It's all right," he told them. "I'm giving myself up."

The young priest was over near the door, looking younger than ever, ridiculously young. Martin went toward him, pushing among the policemen.

"Father," he said, thinking: I am able to speak at last. I am able to accuse myself, to admit. "I want to go to confession."

They went together into the parlor where the old priest lay, and Mandel followed them, standing self-consciously at the door. Twilight was deepening over the flowers, the candles, shadowing the old, fleshy, arranged face.

"You won't mind," Mandel said.

"Oh, I won't mind," the boy said, and mumbled softly in the atmosphere of death, thinking: this is peace. The young priest cleared his throat uncomfortably; Mandel tried to look unobtrusive by the draperies.

"They'll let me go to the funeral, won't they?" Martin said at the end, looking from the priest to the detective. "They'll let me out? It's going to be a big funeral."